The
SURVIVALIST
(Frontier Justice)

8/18/14

The
SURVIVALIST
(Frontier Justice)

Arthur T. Bradley, Ph.D.

The Survivalist
(Frontier Justice)

Author: Arthur T. Bradley, Ph.D.

Email: arthur@disasterpreparer.com

Website: http://disasterpreparer.com

Illustrations used throughout the book are privately owned and copyright protected. Special thanks are extended to Siobhan Gallagher for editing, Marites Bautista for print layout, Nikola Nevenov for illustrations and cover design, and Joe Hobart for his guidance regarding amateur radios.

Library of Congress Control Number: 2013905437

ISBN 10: 148274631X
ISBN 13: 978-1482746310

Printed in the United States of America

FOREWORD

L ike every novel, the work herein is the stuff of fiction; adventure and escapism are its underlying elements. With that said, the story is not as farfetched as many would think. While it is highly unlikely that the world will suddenly end tomorrow as the result of a pandemic, it is not impossible. There are numerous viruses that are mutations away from decimating the human race, including SARS, Ebola, and the avian flu. Even as this book is going to print, there are reports of both a new strain of avian flu, as well as a deadly "SARS-like" virus that may be transmitted from person to person.

Viruses are quite diverse with over 100 million different types known to exist. In fact, there are more viruses on this planet than all other life combined. They can remain viable even under the worst possible conditions and have been found under the polar ice caps, in hydrothermal vents, and even in salt lakes. Consider that a single liter of sea water contains over ten billion viruses. There is simply no escaping these cell-destroying, self-replicating particles.

The list of illnesses caused by viruses is long and varied, including the common cold, influenza, measles, cholera, smallpox, HIV, and hepatitis. Throughout history, mankind's existence has been repeatedly threatened by viruses. Many don't realize that smallpox, which has thankfully now been eradicated, killed about 300 million people in the twentieth century alone. Another 75 million people have been infected with HIV, of which roughly 35 million have died from AIDS.

Modern medicine has developed vaccinations against many viruses, but new mutations are discovered every year. If an untreatable virus was to mutate such that it could be passed through airborne transmission, the number of dead could reach into the billions before a treatment could be developed and administered. Consider yourself warned that the world is not as safe as we would all like to believe.

*"Every dog, we are told, has his day,
unless there are more dogs than days."*

William Barclay "Bat" Masterson
November 26, 1853 – October 25, 1921

Mankind had become a parasite in the strictest definition of the word: an organism that grows, feeds, and is sheltered on a different organism while contributing nothing to the survival of its host. In other words, it had become a professional dinner guest.

Dr. Victor Jarvis had this revelation while flying home from the annual *Conference of Molecular Virology* held in Los Angeles every fall. He stared out the airplane window and marveled at the endless sprawling cities, each with roads and railways stretching out in every direction like the pseudopods of an amoeba. Factories spewed toxic pollutants into the air and sea; forests were clear-cut to the point where the planet's life-supporting atmosphere was in danger; and the ground itself was defiled in search of precious metals and fuels.

Like a virus, man would continue to replicate himself and his associated destruction until the host would eventually die. No corner of the globe would be unaffected, from the deepest oceans to the tallest mountains. Mankind was ever expanding, ever consuming. It was on a course not only to destroy the land and deplete its resources, but also to subjugate or annihilate every living species on the planet. While Dr. Jarvis was not a religious man, he knew with certainty that this revelation was beyond a mere understanding. It was an undeniable truth, an epiphany that had been voiced by the supernatural. Whether it was God, an unknown cosmic power, or simply Mother Earth whispering in his ear, he could not be certain.

Moments of clarity are rare for anyone, and Dr. Jarvis understood that if he did not act quickly and decisively, this newfound truth risked becoming clouded by rationalization and excuse. It was perfectly clear what must be done. Someone must destroy the parasite. For many, such a task would prove utterly impossible, a vain effort that would end with little, if any, effect. The madness would march on to its undeniable end with the attempted intervention yielding nothing more than a footnote in mankind's apocalyptic history. Dr. Jarvis, however, was not one of the many, nor had he ever been. Gifted beyond most people's understanding, he was a pioneer in microbiology and virology, a true genius by any measure.

Along with his prowess came a unique access to the cure. And it truly was a cure: an end to the spread of a deadly disease. He fully accepted that perhaps he could not kill the parasite entirely, as life always finds ways to adapt and survive, but he could at least retard its growth long enough to give the Earth and its other natural species time to recover.

He glanced around the airplane as if to subliminally announce his idea for everyone to consider. Children poked at one another for their turn to use a handheld game console. An old woman carefully penned a letter to the family she had just visited. Businessmen smiled and drank small bottles of vodka while talking about growing opportunities in Latin America. Others napped, content to let time pass quietly. If his plan were to come to fruition, these people would all likely suffer and die through no particular fault of their own. Dr. Jarvis held no malice toward these or any other specific individuals. Like a single *virion*, they neither understand nor cared that they were part of a larger destructive organism. That ignorance, however, could not serve as either excuse or justification for their salvation.

Should he be discovered, his actions would be considered murderous, and perhaps even those of a madman. Dr. Jarvis was confident, however, that future generations (should there be any) would recognize him as the bravest of men, one with a vision that was both necessary and noble. He was, after all, acting out of a broader sense of duty; from what some might even recognize as love.

As with countless experiments that he had conducted in the past, Dr. Jarvis would take his time considering the steps needed for a successful outcome. There were four critical components: a viral agent, a host, broad exposure, and time for the agent to spread. Not only did he know of the perfect agent, he knew precisely how to gain access. As for the host, no one but himself could be trusted. He certainly couldn't ask another to bear such a burden. The issues of exposure and time were closely linked. If the exposure was too limited, or if an early warning was provided, the parasite known as mankind would simply retreat until the threat had passed. Likewise, if the virus manifested too quickly, it would be discovered and contained before it achieved its full potential.

He looked down at a glossy brochure he had picked up from the conference. It was for the upcoming *Global Influenza Research and Development Symposium* that was to be held in Washington, DC, in March. He hadn't planned on attending, but it was too perfect of an opportunity to pass up. Members from more than forty countries would be in attendance. Nearly all of them would have returned home before the infection could be discovered. With careful delivery, he could ensure a global distribution while only having to make a single appearance himself. Surely it would be one of history's greatest ironies that the mechanism for the outbreak would be hundreds of experts in the area of virology, but, as he had said many times, the world was not without a sense of humor.

Dr. Jarvis settled back in his seat and stared out the window, a slight smile touching his lips. He imagined a world without mankind's footprint, its pollution, its greed or barbarism. Such a world was not one to be feared but rather to be embraced. He would make such a world possible for all those who remained. He would kill the parasite.

Deputy U.S. Marshal Mason Raines turned his black Ford F150 truck up the long dirt driveway. The morning air was crisp, and fog steamed out from the thick green foliage like the breath of a sleeping dragon. He carefully navigated a full quarter mile up the drive, steering around deep ruts that had resulted from a year of unusually heavy rain. Arriving at a large metal gate, he stepped from the warmth of his truck and unlocked the chains holding it in place. A gentle push sent the heavy barrier swinging open. The simple action reminded him of the countless times he had sat in a truck very similar to his own, watching his father open the same gate. The nostalgia left Mason imagining his father there with him, as if time had folded over to allow the past and present to briefly coexist.

He pulled the truck forward a few paces and climbed out again to close the gate behind him. He wondered why he even bothered. The turn off to his property was difficult to see, and other than the occasional teenagers looking for a make-out spot, there was very little chance of anyone disturbing his remote getaway. Even if they did, what trouble could they cause? Vandalism perhaps, but that didn't seem likely. Most people were decent enough. More likely, they would simply let themselves into his cabin and enjoy a weekend in the mountains. For all he knew, the occasional unannounced visitor might even do the place a little good.

The cabin was distant enough from Mason's daily routine that he would have let the place go if circumstances had not dictated otherwise. With his father doing fifteen years in the Talladega Federal Correctional Institution for manslaughter and his mother living with her sister on an Amish farm in rural New York, the duty of maintaining the family's mountain retreat had fallen squarely on his shoulders.

More than just duty brought him to the cabin. Mason's job as a firearms instructor at the Federal Law Enforcement Training Center (FLETC) in Glynco, Georgia was an endless routine of high-stress training, one that he gladly escaped when offered the chance to breathe the fresh mountain air and enjoy a little peace and quiet.

He drove the final hundred yards and parked on a small gravel lot directly in front of the cabin. Built in the truest tradition of log cabins, his father had constructed it from huge trees cut from the surrounding property. From the outside, it looked more like a small cavalry outpost hardened to protect against hostile Apaches than a weekend mountain getaway.

As Mason approached the cabin, he reached out and rubbed a wooden eagle that sat like a protective totem to one side of the porch. His mother had fancied herself a bit of an undiscovered artist, and the eagle was one of her many contributions to their family retreat. Like those who suffer from compulsive behavior disorders, Mason had an almost uncontrollable urge to touch the eagle each time he went into the home, especially when he had been away for some time. Perhaps it stemmed from a fond remembrance of his mother, or perhaps it was just a simple request for divine luck, similar to rubbing the belly of a Buddha statue.

The cabin's door was a massive slab of oak, one rivaling the castle drawbridges of medieval England. His mother had added a large metal knocker in the shape of a monkey's fist, saying that, without it, someone would have to bloody their knuckles for anyone inside to hear them. The point ultimately proved irrelevant since the cabin remained unknown to any but their immediate family. It was a small secret in a world where few secrets remained. As far as anyone from the nearby towns knew, the land was simply another tract of undeveloped property that one day might be cleared for trees or mined for ore.

Mason entered the cabin, and the familiar smell of wood and dust welcomed him like the scent of a mother's freshly baked cookies. It had been nearly six months since he had last stepped foot in the cabin, and, as with all homes, time and nature were its worst enemies. A few small items had been knocked over, almost certainly by raccoons searching for food. Despite his many efforts to keep the structure well sealed and protected from the elements, raccoons and the occasional squirrel or bat invariably found their way in. He took down the heavy wooden shutters and opened a few windows. The temperatures in late March were still chilly in the morning, but the fresh air brought life back to the sleepy cabin.

He walked around to the back of the building and removed a heavy tarp from a large downdraft gasification generator. The unique electromechanical system consisted of a pressure vessel, burner unit, gas-burning turbine, and a maze of copper plumbing that tied it all together. Mason took great pride in having successfully built the unit two years earlier. It could be fueled by a variety of biomass products, including timber and crops. He had picked up most of the parts from a salvage yard, and, as such, the twenty-kilowatt beast looked as if it belonged in the belly of a Navy destroyer.

He piled a full load of dried timber into the main vessel and lit it from below. Within minutes chemical reactions would begin producing *syngas*, a composition of hydrogen and carbon monoxide. That gas would in turn be cleaned and then burned in the electricity-generating turbine. The entire energy conversion process was remarkably clean and self-sustaining.

Next to the generator was a large burn box that his father had used to heat both the house and the water. It would burn most anything from wood to garbage, and Mason could remember many an early morning loading the box with freshly cut firewood. He was a bit ashamed to admit that he hadn't even fired it up since installing a more modern furnace and hot water heater that ran off the gasification-generated electricity. Still, just looking at the heavy metal box reassured him that the cabin would remain warm throughout the harshest of winters, even if his prized generator was to fail.

Mason's next stop was the main breaker box where he switched on the power. He spent a few minutes checking the motion-detecting flood lights mounted at each corner of the cabin. While they could certainly be useful against potential intruders, they were handiest at keeping away bears and other creatures in search of food. Doing a quick inspection of the inside of the cabin revealed little damage, save for a couple of lamps that had been knocked over and some fresh scratches on the doorframe. He checked the refrigerator, and it appeared to be cooling down just fine.

Returning to his truck, he retrieved several bags of food and drinks. While he kept a full year's supply of prepackaged freeze-dried food stored in a locked pantry in the cabin, he didn't like to use his food cache for anything less than a true emergency. With a shelf life of at least thirty years, the food would very possibly outlive him.

Once Mason situated the food in the cupboards and refrigerator, he checked the water supply. The spigot in the kitchen sputtered and spat, but eventually ran clear, clean water. The generator powered a submersible pump, which in turn kept the cabin's thousand-gallon water tank full. He had changed the pump just last year, and had also installed a cast iron hand crank in case the electric unit should ever fail. The water table wasn't particularly deep, and if needed, he could refill the tank by hand with a hard day's work.

Having taken care of food, water, and electricity, Mason turned his attention to what really mattered—fishing. He pulled out a painted green tackle box that had once been his father's and began sorting through brightly colored lures and jigs. Beautiful cutthroat trout could be pulled all day long from a stream not more than a ten-minute hike away. For three weeks, there would be no phone, no television, no internet, and, most important, no excuses from students who couldn't place their shots in a target shaped like a large bowling pin. Just fresh fish, a little target practice in the backyard, and a chance to catch up on a pile of books he had put off reading. Mason was determined that these were going to be the best three weeks of his life.

ॐ ◌

Mason sat up, covered in a heavy sweat. He struggled to recall the dream that had left his heart racing and hands trembling. Nothing specific came to mind. As with most dreams, it was gone as quickly as the wisp of a passing perfume. He considered lying back down but knew that sleep would elude him until he managed to clear any remnants of the dream from the corners of his mind. Seeing no other choice, he crawled out of bed, relieved himself in the adjacent bathroom, and brewed a cup of fresh decaf coffee.

Grabbing a large double-barreled shotgun that had once been his father's, he stepped out onto the front porch and sat in a rocking chair. With the heavy weapon resting across his lap like a ballplayer's favorite bat, he stared out at the dark, listening to the sounds of life all around him. Owls chimed to one another. Raccoons scrambled about, causing trouble everywhere they went. Bats flicked across the sky, enjoying a feast of nocturnal insects. Crickets and countless other bugs chirped and flitted, filling the air with an endless cacophony of noises. Mason sipped his coffee for a few minutes, enjoying his fragile place in the complex world around him.

A gunshot sounded. Then a second, and a third. They were far enough away that Mason didn't even stop rocking in his chair. It could easily have been a mile, maybe even a little farther. Probably hunters out chasing raccoons, he thought. While Mason had no particular love for the critters, he didn't like the thought of a pack of dogs running down the animals until their masters could finally catch up and finish the job with a shotgun.

In his seven years with the Marshal Service, he had been forced to fire his weapon on six different occasions, an unusually high number to be sure. In each of those cases, however, his opponent had been armed, either with a rifle, handgun, or, in one case, a machete. Taking a life under those circumstances seemed distinctly different than butchering an animal in the middle of the night for nothing more than its pelt.

Despite his indignation, he made no move to question the illegal hunting. Not only was it unacceptably dangerous to do so, it was also a fight that he was unwilling to enter. The world had its predators and prey. Man was fortunate enough to be at the top of the food chain in most environments, and, when he wasn't, he felt the sharp bite of whatever it was that held authority over him. Such was the way of the world. Mason wondered if one day that same world might decide that man had held the top post for long enough.

President Rosalyn Glass stood staring out the window of the Oval Office. The VH-60N helicopter, known as Marine One, whipped the grass with its massive blades as it slowly descended onto the White House South Lawn. They would be coming for her soon.

She held a cup of tea close to her face, the steam slowly rising to condense on her glasses. Her hands trembled, and her heart pounded so violently that she wondered if others might actually be able to hear it. She tried to steady herself by sipping the hot brew, and it immediately burned her lips. She lowered the cup and licked at the tender flesh. Pain, she thought, not just for me; enough for everyone.

She replayed the conversation that she'd had with her Chief of Staff less than a half-hour earlier, a conversation that would forever change her life and those of billions of others.

Tom Barnes stepped into the Oval Office and announced himself.

"Madam President."

"What is it?" she asked, stepping from behind the Resolute, the 19th century desk that had served nearly every president since John F. Kennedy.

His ashen face betrayed the severity of his message.

"Ma'am, there's been an incident."

"What kind of incident?"

He stared at her, unable or perhaps just unwilling, to put words to the catastrophe.

She raised an eyebrow. "Talk to me, Tom. How bad is it?" They had dealt with a host of emergencies during her first two years of presidency, and she had never seen him so shaken.

"There's been—" his voice faltered. He tried again. "There's been a release of a viral contagion."

President Glass moved to the sofa and sat. She struggled to keep her composure. "Tell me."

Her Chief of Staff sat in a chair across from the couch, as he always did.

"The incident occurred at the Army's Biological Warfare Lab in Fort Detrick, Maryland. We don't have all the details yet," he said, shaking his head, "but what we do know is that a small amount of a viral agent was inhaled by a researcher."

"*What exactly was inhaled?*" she asked, horrified by the thought of anyone being exposed to a biological weapon.

"*It's known as Superpox-99. The symptoms are similar to those of smallpox: blisters, respiratory distress, blindness, limb deformation. It's as bad as you can imagine.*" He looked down to study his hands. "*Worse than you can imagine.*"

"*Why the hell were they working with something like that?*" Even as she asked the question, she knew there was little point in pretending righteous outrage. Despite the country's public signing of the Biological and Toxin Weapons Convention in 1972, advanced research had continued to identify and isolate a superbug that might prove the ultimate deterrent and thus tip the balance of modern warfare.

Tom understood that she didn't expect an answer, and so he offered none.

"*How deadly is this thing, Tom? Give me numbers to work with.*"

"*As the name implies, if it's not treated within the first couple of days, about ninety-nine percent of those infected die within two weeks.*"

"*My Lord,*" she said, covering her mouth. "*And it's contagious?*"

"*Yes, Madam President, highly contagious.*"

"*Please tell me it requires physical contact,*" she pleaded.

He stared at her and shook his head.

"*It can be passed through airborne transmission. People wouldn't have to be any closer than we are right now.*"

President Glass noticed that with the addition of each horrific detail, her Chief of Staff's voice began to sound more and more distant, as if emanating from an old phonograph player.

"*I don't care what it takes,*" she said, "*the National Guard, the entire armed forces—you contain this thing. Seal off Fort Detrick. Hell, seal off the entire state of Maryland if you need to. Just contain this thing. Do you hear me?*"

Tom Barnes shook his head again.

"*No ma'am.*"

Her face grew splotchy, as she could no longer control her nerves.

"*No? Why not?*"

"*If we'd known sooner, maybe. Now . . .*" He let the words hang in the air like a promise that had been broken. "*Now, it's too late.*"

"*What do you mean 'if we'd known sooner?' When did this happen?*"

He pressed back against the chair, hoping to create more distance between them. His eyes filled with tears.

"*Seven days ago.*"

"*What!*" President Glass leaped to her feet. "*Why wasn't I told?*"

"*No one was, Madam President. The researcher didn't report his infection. In fact, he went to great lengths to hide it.*"

"Are you telling me this was an act of domestic terrorism?"

He shrugged. *"There's no way to know for sure at this point, but, yes, it's possible."*

"No, no, no," she said, more to herself than to him. *"Seven days?"*

"Yes ma'am."

"And the researcher? Where is he now?"

"He's in a quarantine unit at Johns Hopkins in Baltimore."

"We need to question him, find out where he's been, who he might have infected."

"I'm afraid that's not possible. He's unable to speak and is expected to die within a few hours." The Chief of Staff pulled a glossy photograph from his jacket pocket and passed it to her.

After a quick glance, President Glass let the photo fall to the floor.

"He doesn't even look human."

"No ma'am," he said, picking up the photo.

She sat for nearly a minute without speaking.

"What are we going to do, Tom?"

He shrugged again.

"What we can. We've alerted the CDC, FEMA, Homeland Security, and most other agencies. The Joint Chiefs are taking protective measures to keep our military viable."

"And the broader civilian population? Can we provide a vaccination or at least some antiviral treatment?"

"There is no vaccine, Madam President. The CDC will work around the clock to develop one, but that will take weeks or months. As for the antiviral medicines, the generals are requesting the nation's full stockpile."

"All of it?"

"Yes ma'am. There's barely enough to treat a million people. Even if they begin treating every soldier on active or reserve duty, most will still die."

"What are you telling me, Tom?" she asked with a nervous smile. *"That the world is about to end?"*

Tom Barnes closed his eyes and began to weep.

"Yes, Madam President. That's exactly what I'm telling you."

The Chief of Staff had told President Glass that her husband and eleven-year-old daughter would be temporarily quarantined in a secure underground facility in Colorado. The president herself would be immediately transported to the Mount Weather Emergency Operations Center in Bluemont, Virginia. Despite everyone's best efforts, however, there was no guarantee that any of them would survive. Precautions would be taken: protective suits, careful screening of those with whom they came into contact, and immediate dosing with antiviral medicines. But none of that would matter much if they had already been infected. Infection all but ensured death. Ninety-nine percent if left untreated. Slightly better than that if carefully monitored, but still, the odds were far from being in anyone's favor.

President Glass wasn't sure what was eating at her the most, that the world that she knew was ending, or that it was doing so on her watch. She had failed the country. Probably the entire world. If the experts were right, the planet would be systematically wiped clean of nearly all of mankind in a few short weeks. Save for the remotest regions, every corner of the planet would be decimated. Most people would never know how or where it had started, and by the time suspicions could be confirmed, it would be too late.

Placing her cup of tea on a small table, President Glass did the only thing she could. She dropped to both knees and began to pray.

Dear God, in this time of great suffering, I ask only one thing. Please spare my little girl.

For three relaxing weeks, Mason enjoyed the isolation of the Blue Ridge Mountains from the comfort of his family's cabin. He completed a host of fix-it projects, caught more fish than he could eat, and practiced with a 1911 semi-automatic pistol. The handgun, a Wilson Combat Tactical Supergrade in .45 caliber, was arguably one of the finest pistols currently in production. Unfortunately, it also was also one of the most expensive. Marshal Leroy Tucker, a friend and avid gun buff, had loaned it to him to try out over his vacation. With more than five hundred rounds passing through the match grade barrel while in his brief care, that was exactly what Mason had done.

Mason was normally required to carry the Marshal Service's standard issue Glock .40 because of its ease in handling and high reliability. He was surprised at how walking around with the Supergrade on his hip felt so natural. It was certainly a more beautiful weapon, albeit a bit more complicated to operate in a gunfight. The thrill of carrying such a fine firearm would be short-lived, however, as he had to return it to Marshal Tucker the following Monday.

It took him nearly a full hour to secure the cabin, locking the windows and doors, hanging the shutters, latching the cabinets to prevent unwanted four-legged visitors, covering the generator and wood pile, and tying down everything outside that he didn't want blown halfway across the county. He loaded his bags into the back of the truck, including a few days of extra food and drinks that he hadn't consumed. When everything was loaded and secured, he took one last trip around the cabin to make sure that nothing had been overlooked. Once he deemed the property ready to weather another six months without attention, Mason climbed in his truck and started the seven-hour drive back to his apartment in northern Brunswick.

The drive from the cabin to his first coffee stop in Boone started on a narrow scenic road that saw very little traffic in the offseason. Cracks and potholes ensured that no one got in too big of a hurry. Giant trees stretched their limbs out over the road, their protective canopies letting in only the occasional slivers of fresh sunlight. Mason gave the drive his full attention because deer, possums, and the occasional flock of wild turkeys were frequent early morning jaywalkers.

He was surprised to come across an old blue Chevrolet pickup sitting halfway off the small road, its wheels resting in deep ruts left by logging trucks. His first thought was that hikers had braved the early morning chill to see Silver Stretch Falls, a scenic waterfall that spilled into the Watauga Reservoir. He slowed and pulled around the truck, instinctively glancing into the cab as he passed. While he caught only a glimpse, what he saw was something more suited to a drug-infested ghetto than a quiet country road.

He hit the brakes hard, stopping about ten feet in front of the Chevrolet. Leaving the engine running, he stepped out of his truck and took a look around. Nothing moved, and the only sound was the wind whistling through the trees as if a mountain giant was working out a tune on his favorite harmonica.

Parting his sport coat so that his badge was visible on his belt, he placed his hand on the grip of the Supergrade and slowly approached the truck. He was careful to maintain a clear view of the windshield and both doors because, despite the finality of what he had seen, it didn't mean there wasn't still some danger lurking within. He personally knew several peace officers who had been killed or injured as the result of letting their guard down when approaching a crime scene.

As he stepped up to the driver's side window, the carnage inside came into full view. Three bodies lay sprawled across the cloth bucket seats. The driver, a man in his mid-fifties, had a gunshot wound to his right temple. His head lay forward against the steering wheel, a large spray of blood and brains peppering the windshield. To his right sat two women, one about his age and another perhaps thirty years younger. Both were shot through the heart. Three shots: three dead.

Not wanting to disturb the crime scene, Mason left the vehicle doors closed and worked his way cautiously around the truck, looking in the various windows for clues as to what had happened. He spotted a .38 revolver dangling from the right hand of the lifeless driver. Murder suicide? It certainly appeared so. What it didn't explain was why the two women hadn't put up a fight. The shots were precise, and there were dark circular powder burns on their shirts, indicating that they had allowed their attacker to carefully place the pistol against their chests before firing. The evidence pointed to a triple suicide, which was extremely rare.

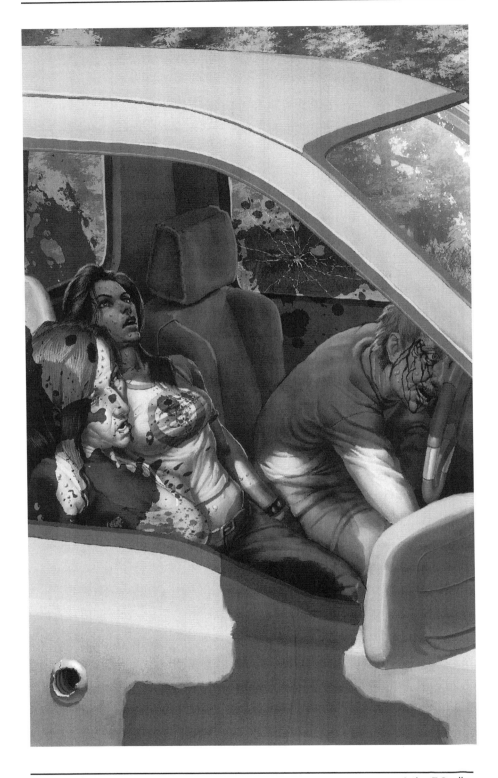

The bodies had already passed through rigor mortis and were lying limp on the seats, like noodles that had boiled too long. Soon, gases would build up in their gastrointestinal and respiratory systems, causing skin to swell and blood to spew from their noses. Eventually the skin would rupture along their arms and legs, splitting open to spill their gory contents. The fact that they hadn't yet started to swell meant that they'd been dead for less than two or three days.

Mason checked around the pickup to see if there were any footprints to indicate that someone else might have been involved. Everywhere he looked, the ground was undisturbed. For whatever reason, these people had brought about their own bloody end. He released his weapon and walked back to his truck. As he climbed back in, it occurred to him that he now knew the source of the shots he had heard the other night. It had been something much more disturbing than simple midnight poachers.

He clicked on his two-way police radio, but, surprisingly, only static sounded. He pressed the microphone button and said, "This is Deputy U.S. Marshal Raines requesting assistance, over."

There was no reply.

The radio was a modern wideband digital transceiver, so there was no manual channel control. Everything was automatic. It either worked or it didn't. His transmission was frequency coded such that any law enforcement officer within range would hear it. The complete lack of activity over the air could only mean that his radio was inoperable.

A quick check of his cell phone revealed that it too had no service available. That, however, wasn't particularly surprising given his remote location. Cell coverage was spotty at best in the mountains and could remain that way almost all the way down to Boone. His best bet was probably just to drive to town and contact the local police. The biggest risk was that someone might come upon the crime scene and inadvertently destroy key evidence. Given that it appeared to be a mass suicide, however, even if that happened, it probably wouldn't change the outcome.

Just to be on the safe side, he walked around the pickup one final time and snapped a few photos with the camera on his cell phone. Once Mason was sure that he had enough evidence for local authorities to get to the bottom of what had happened, he tossed the phone onto the passenger seat and continued his drive to Boone.

For the next ten minutes, Mason didn't see a single car on the road. That in itself was a little surprising because the area was frequented by outdoorsmen hoping to pull in a few trout as well as young mountain bikers hitting the trails.

As he came around a long bend that opened up to a popular scenic stop, he discovered two cars involved in a head-on collision. The larger vehicle, a white Lincoln Town Car that looked as if it belonged at the yacht club, clearly got the better of a much smaller Honda compact. The windows were wet with condensation No one stood beside either car; neither were there any police or tow trucks present.

Mason stopped his truck in the center of the road, blocking off any potential traffic that might approach from behind. A quick check of his cell phone showed that service was still unavailable. He climbed out of his truck and approached the accident with a disconcerting feeling of dèjá vu. Given that the collision must have happened hours earlier, he was surprised that the accident had not yet been discovered and reported to the highway patrol or local authorities.

The Town Car had only a twisted bumper and broken headlight, and no one was sitting inside. The driver's door was wide open, suggesting that he may have quickly fled the scene, as was often the case when an accident involved a drunk driver. The Honda had not fared nearly as well. The entire front end was crumpled, and a large puddle of antifreeze and oil had pooled beneath it like blood from an injured warhorse. Two people were sitting in the front seats. Both were badly mangled, and there was no doubt that they were stone-cold dead. From the awkward positioning of the bodies, Mason assumed that they were still in rigor mortis, which aligned well with his conclusion that the accident had occurred sometime in the night.

He rubbed his chin, mulling over what he was seeing. In all his years, he had never come across two scenes within minutes of one another where people were lying not only dead but unattended. It was either a strange coincidence, or more likely, the two were somehow connected. As he had done at the previous scene, he walked around the vehicles to ensure he hadn't missed anything important. As he came around the Lincoln, he nearly stumbled over another body lying beside the rear wheel.

It was of a woman in her late thirties, dressed in an expensive-looking gray skirt and white silk blouse. The cause of her death was difficult to determine. Her face and arms were covered in large, pus-filled boils that early decomposition couldn't hide. There was also bloody foam on her lips that looked as if she had aspirated her favorite fruit salad. Her eyes were open, and the whites were laced with a network of red streaks caused by petechial hemorrhaging. Suffocation seemed to be the probable cause of death except for the fact that, from the knee down, her right leg was completely missing. A long trail of blood led up into the woods. Animals of some sort had obviously gotten to her. Whether that happened while she was alive or dead was difficult for him to say.

Perhaps even more disturbing than her grotesque appearance was the repugnant odor that outgassed from her body. Mason knew too well the putrid stink of decaying bodies, but this was something different. It was more of a rancid smell, and it made him want to cover his nose and spit the saliva from his mouth. While he was certainly no bacteriologist, he had smelled enough curdled milk to know when something had gone bad.

He returned to his truck, walking slowly and methodically. Three people shot to death, a car crash with bodies lying unattended, and a potentially infectious disease the likes of which he had not seen before. Having been a soldier and lawman for most of his adult life, Mason considered himself hardened to death and violence. But, taken together, the bloody scenes felt surreal, as if civilization's normal checks and balances were being tested.

He tried the two-way radio again, but the airwaves remained silent. He reached up and held his cell phone out the window with the hopes of picking up even spotty reception. Nothing. Mason shook his head in disbelief. The universe was clearly conspiring against him. He flipped on the blue light sitting on his dash, popped his truck into drive, and started down the mountain road with a newfound sense of urgency. It was time to get some help.

When Mason turned from Buckeye Road, a small rural stretch that led up to hiking trails and weekend getaways, onto Highway 321, his first thought was that there had been a huge accident. Hundreds of vehicles were scattered along the roadway, facing every possible direction, as if they had been tossed into the air as part of a colossal game of pick-up sticks. Several had crashed, or perhaps been pushed, into the deep gullies that lined the sides and center of the thoroughfare. Cars, trucks, tractor-trailers, emergency vehicles, and even a school bus were mixed into the automotive bedlam.

Mason stopped his truck and paused a moment to try to grasp what he was witnessing. It was an impossible sight, one that he found hard to accept even when seeing it with his own eyes. It was as if thousands of people had attempted to flee some supernatural evil only to be caught in its clutches on this cursed stretch of freeway. The war zones that he had experienced in Iraq held nothing over the destruction before him now.

Not a single person walked along the highway. A few cars still had their headlights glowing dimly, but, other than the occasional spinning wheel of an overturned car, nothing moved. The roadway was utterly lifeless, as if mankind had been suddenly scratched from the planet, leaving only the scars of its technology behind. Mason could only think of a single word to describe the chaos that he was seeing: *Armageddon.*

Not knowing what else to do, he shut off his truck and got out. His first steps were tentative as he unconsciously tested the asphalt to see if it might suddenly collapse and drop him into an invisible abyss. No such doom befell him. On the contrary, the air was calm and the scene strangely peaceful. Only the occasional creak of a settling vehicle broke the silence.

He walked slowly toward a small camper trailer that had partially overturned. The passenger door was wedged open, and the corpse of a fat man was leaning out, dangling from his seatbelt like a condemned man from the gallows' noose. Mason circled around to the front of the camper to get a better view of the cab. Another man rested behind the steering wheel, also quite dead. Both were covered in the same blisters that he had seen on the woman lying beside the Town Car.

He checked several other vehicles, and nearly all of them contained decaying corpses with similar symptoms. Something terrible had killed these people. Most of the cars were facing away from Boone, but there were also some heading into the small town. Whatever had killed them was so widespread that they hadn't known which direction offered salvation.

Mason made his way back to his truck and shut off the flashing blue light on the dash. He started to reach for his phone again but surrendered to the fact that it wasn't going to work. There was only one logical explanation for why he didn't have radio or cellular phone service. The entire area had been affected by some sort of pandemic or biochemical attack. That in turn must have led to the loss of infrastructure services. The only other possibility he could think of was that the authorities had sealed the area and intentionally cut off all forms of communication to prevent those who were contaminated from calling out for help. No one wanted those 911 calls played back for years to come.

Mason had a long list of questions that needed answering. How widespread was the pandemic or attack? What methods were being used to contain it? Was it airborne, and, if so, was he in danger? What steps could be taken to prevent infection? Had a quarantine zone been set up to prevent the spread of the illness? And if so, how could he safely exit it?

He swung the truck around and headed back the way he had come. Everything he needed to get answers was back at the cabin.

By the time Mason arrived at the cabin, his mind was racing like a rookie trying to win his first NASCAR title. What he needed most was information. He had repeatedly tried the two-way radio and cell phone, both of which had failed him miserably. Now it was time to broaden his reach. He hurried around back and once again fired up the generator. Then he went inside and climbed a ladder to a small upstairs loft where his radio equipment was set up. He had been a licensed amateur radio operator for several years and knew from experience that, under the right conditions, one-hundred-watt broadcasts such as his could skip halfway around the world. Reaching out to those beyond the area of infection should be quite easy.

He switched on the radio and checked the power level and antenna selection. Everything was a go. He tuned to a frequency in the 20-meter band that was active during emergencies, hoping to hear traffic. When he didn't hear any transmissions, he said, "This is KB4VXP. Is anyone listening on this frequency? I'm looking for information on the pandemic."

He waited for a response. When none came, he repeated his call for help.

After his second transmission, a voice said, "Who is this?" The voice was that of a young woman. She wasn't following standard Ham jargon.

Mason keyed his microphone.

"This is KB4VXP. What is your call sign, over?"

"I . . . I don't know. This was my husband's radio." She sounded close to having an emotional breakdown.

"Okay. No problem. Take it slow. Where are you broadcasting from?"

"I'm in Ukiah."

"Where's Ukiah?" he asked, wondering if she was even in the States.

"Northern California. Where are you? Are you close? My son and I need help."

Mason didn't like what he was hearing. Surely, the pandemic or attack hadn't reached all the way to the West Coast.

"Tell me what's going on. I'm listening."

"They're dead," she cried.

"Who's dead?"

"Everyone's dead!"

Mason took a deep breath.

"What's your name, dear?"

There was a slight pause.

"Kathryn. Kate. I'm Kate Battens."

"All right, Kate, I'm Mason. Relax, okay? Let's just talk. We'll figure this out together. Tell me what's going on."

"Right," she said, her voice steadying. "We're in trouble here. Nearly everyone around us is dead, and no one has come to help."

"How did they die?" he asked, already knowing the answer.

"The virus. Superpox-99. Only my son and I survived."

Mason had never heard of Superpox-99, but he wasn't going to lose his only link to the outside world by having her question his usefulness.

"How many are dead in Ukiah? In California?"

"They're all dead. My neighbors. My husband. My co-workers. My pastor. They're all dead," she repeated, her voice rising again.

"Has Superpox-99 affected the major cities? Los Angeles? San Francisco?"

"I think so," she answered. "We have no TV. No radio. No power or even water. I'm running this radio using my husband's generator. Please, we need help desperately."

Mason considered the implications of what she was telling him. He reminded himself that she could be wrong. People who were in disaster areas often made assumptions about things that later proved untrue. Maybe the virus wasn't as widespread as she claimed.

Then again, maybe it was.

Before he could reply, another voice came over the radio.

"This is WA4RTF. Who is transmitting, over?"

"This is KB4VXP, Deputy Marshal Mason Raines." Normally, he wouldn't have identified himself as a law enforcement officer when transmitting over amateur radio, but given the circumstances, it felt right.

"It's good to hear your voice, Marshal. I'm Jack Atkins. Any chance you can provide an update on the spread of the virus? Also, please relay your location and conditions, over."

"I'm near Boone, North Carolina. The virus has definitely hit here. Where are you, Jack?"

Kate suddenly cut in.

"Jack, are you close to California? We need rescue. Please, my son is only eight."

Jack took a moment before answering.

"Ma'am, I'm sorry, but you're nearly three thousand miles from me. I'm in Gloucester, Virginia. No way that I can reach you. Not in time anyway."

"Listen Kate," said Mason, "we'll get you help. Just hang in there. Do either of you know the state of the country? Has the National Guard been deployed? What areas remain unaffected?"

Jack came back on.

"Marshal, I was hoping you could tell us that."

When Mason didn't answer, Jack continued. "From what I've been able to determine, this thing's global. I have yet to find anyone in an unaffected area. As for the National Guard, I imagine they died right alongside everyone else. How is it you're out of the loop on all this, Marshal?"

"I've been in the mountains for a few weeks and am just now seeing the damage."

"I'd say you picked one hell of an opportune time to get away from other people."

"Does the virus require physical contact?" Mason asked, thinking about his encounters with those lying dead on the road.

"No. It can definitely be passed through the air. Get coughed or spit on by someone infected and you've joined the walking dead."

"Then why didn't I catch it? Or my son?" asked Kate. It was clear from the trembling in her voice that she had been crying again.

"As with every virus, I suppose there are some people with a natural immunity to it. You and your son must be two of the lucky ones, if you want to call it that."

"What about you, Jack?" asked Mason. "Are you immune too?"

"I seriously doubt it. When I saw things going downhill, my wife and I locked ourselves up tight. We haven't left the house in over two weeks. I've been trolling the airwaves ever since, trying to piece things together."

Mason nodded. Jack was someone worth knowing, a *prepper* who'd had enough sense and supplies to hole up and wait things out.

"What do you know about the virus? Is there a treatment? A vaccination?"

"I'm pretty sure that the initial reports over the TV and radio were government-filtered to prevent panicking," replied Jack. "But based on what I'm hearing, it's bad. Real bad. Until I get out, I can't say for sure. As for an antidote or vaccination, I'm not aware of either."

"There was an announcement by the CDC," interjected Kate, "that they were working on a vaccine, but I never heard if they were successful. TV, radio, and the internet all shut down. My guess is there just wasn't time."

"Even if they don't have a vaccine yet, you can bet that scientists are working around the clock in a sealed lab somewhere," said Mason. "Once this thing broke out, they would have put in place emergency protocols to ensure that the nation survived."

"I agree," said Jack. "But it may have been too little too late. Not to sound like a doomsayer, but I think our country is all but dead."

"Listen, both of you, I need help," Kate pleaded. "We're going to die if one of you doesn't help us. Do you understand? My son and I are going to die."

The airway remained silent for several seconds.

Mason considered his options. The best he could do was to offer some advice.

"What are your most pressing needs?"

"Water," she replied quickly. "We've been forced to drink from our neighbor's swimming pool, and it's making us both sick."

"Okay, that one's easy. Start by draining your water heater. That should give you enough for a few weeks if you're careful with it. You can use the pool water to flush your toilet, but use the water in your water heater for drinking and cooking. Do you think you can drain it?"

"I'm . . . I'm not sure. I think so. You hook a hose to the bottom, right?"

"That's right," answered Mason. "Connect a hose to the spigot at the bottom of the tank, and put the other end of the hose into a bucket. Then flip the relief valve at the top of the tank and open the spigot. Some water heaters are a little different, so you may have to play around with it. Just get you and your son some clean water to drink."

"Okay, yes. I can do that. Thank you. Oh, thank you."

"Do you have food?" asked Jack.

"We're scavenging from neighbors' houses. It's awful. People I've known and loved for years are lying dead in their beds or on the floor."

"Kate, you're keeping your son alive," said Mason. "That's what's important right now. Do whatever you need to. Take what you need from those who have passed. They'd want you to do that. Grab food, blankets, fuel, and whatever else you need. When your water heater runs out, drain your neighbors'. You should be able to survive for months by scavenging from those around you."

"I will. But I have to be careful."

"Why? Are you worried about catching the virus?"

"No, it's like Jack said—my son and I must be immune or we'd have caught it from my husband."

"What then?"

"The convicts."

"Convicts? What convicts?"

Jack came on again.

"Marshal, when things got really bad, the president issued an executive order to release prisoners from penal institutions that could no longer be manned."

"Why in the hell would she do that?"

"It was either that or let them die of dehydration and starvation in unattended jail cells. Tough call for anyone."

"She released everyone?"

"No, of course not. The presidential directive only authorized the release of non-violent offenders. Murderers, rapists, and the like were to be consolidated to a few federal prisons in order to make them easier to manage."

"That doesn't sound so bad."

"It might not have been if it had worked as planned. Unfortunately, by the time the order was issued, the prisons were terribly understaffed. With the massive releases and transfers, the plan just fell apart. With over two million people incarcerated, it became impossible to control the situation. Some prisons were emptied; others were overrun by the inmates. A few were just abandoned, leaving prisoners trapped inside."

"Do you have any idea how many convicts were released or escaped?"

"There's no way to know, but from what's being reported over the airways, they're everywhere."

Mason rubbed his temples.

"This just keeps getting better and better."

☙ ❧

Mason spent a good part of the day talking with Jack and Kate. When they finally signed off, everyone agreed to reconnect in two days to share anything new that may have been discovered. While there was still much that he didn't know, Mason had learned that the origin of the virus was still a mystery. Early cases had shown up all over the world, from Russia and

China, to areas across Europe and the Americas. No one yet could explain how it had spread to every corner of the globe so quickly. Given the indiscriminate infection, it was not believed to be a terrorist attack but, rather, Mother Nature flexing her muscle.

It had been reported that Superpox-99 was a modified strain of smallpox that caused similar blistering, respiratory distress, arthritis, and blindness. If left untreated, death was all but certain. Hospitals had been overwhelmed within a few days, and most had to be protected by the National Guard. The emergency medical system eventually failed, as many caregivers became sick or abandoned their posts to tend to their own families.

When the nation's power grid failed, electricity, water, and other utilities were all subsequently lost. Television, radio, and emergency broadcasts fell silent a couple of days later as batteries and generator fuel were depleted. The loss of water and power led to mass exoduses from major cities. Highways became so gridlocked that people took to hiking out with supplies on their backs. In the end, it was unclear how many had survived. Based on what he had seen outside Boone, the number appeared to be quite small.

Mason's thoughts turned to his own family. His father, Tanner Raines, had been incarcerated for more than four years for killing two men outside a bar in Montgomery, Alabama. There was no way to know whether he had he been freed as a result of the president's directive or was lying dead in his cell. If Mason had to guess, he would put money on his father having found a way out of prison. Tanner Raines was not a man who would go quietly into the night. Indeed, when pushed, he could become as violent and unpredictable as a loan shark collecting unpaid debts.

While Mason's first reaction had been one of disbelief when he had heard what the president had done, he also appreciated it on a personal level. She had perhaps given his father a chance at survival. Considering the circumstances, that was as much as anyone could ask. Mason's mother, Grace, was living with her sister in a small Amish community in Cattaraugus County, New York. Her isolated lifestyle, which had once been of some concern to him, was now rather reassuring. There was definitely a possibility that she had escaped the pandemic.

The question was what to do first. On one hand, Mason felt an obligation to check on his family, and, on the other, he had a responsibility to see what remained of the Marshal Service. The Marshals, along with other law enforcement agencies, were surely in need of good men now more than ever. Before either effort could be undertaken, however, he needed to better assess his own predicament. Were things as bad as Kate and Jack had suggested? Was everyone in the neighboring towns dead or dying? Or had the isolated Blue Ridge communities somehow survived the pandemic? Unfortunately, the only way to answer those questions was to leave the safety of his retreat.

Mason went to his bedroom and slid the heavy oak bed to one side. He used a screwdriver to remove several long wood screws that held two floorboards in place. Underneath were a gun case and a large green duffle bag. He lifted both out and placed them on the bed. For a moment, he stared at the case, running his fingertips along the top as if it was a photograph of a recently deceased family member. The time for such weapons had passed in his life, and he was reluctant to admit that such a need existed once again.

He opened the case and removed the Colt M4 assault rifle. The weapon had been a gift from an old Army supply buddy whose life he had saved. It had been almost two years since he had secured the assault rifle under the floorboards of the cabin, but the weapon was still slick with a thick layer of grease. He held it up and looked down the fixed sights. Memories of combat played like an old home movie clicking along frame by frame, the images no longer real but, instead, snapshots of something that could never be completely forgotten.

He pulled the charging handle, set the selector switch to semi-automatic, and squeezed the trigger. A familiar metallic *click* sounded. This was a weapon he trusted, a weapon that had saved his life on more than one occasion. He set the rifle beside him on the bed and untied the heavy drawstring that held the canvas bag closed. Inside were an assortment of cleaning supplies, a stack of thirty-round magazines, and more than a thousand rounds of ammunition. He removed and inspected each item.

When the bag was finally empty, he opened the cleaning kit and went to work on getting the rifle ready for operation. Many things were still unknown, but one thing was for sure. The world had suddenly become a very dangerous place.

Tanner Raines lay on his small bunk, arms folded behind his head, staring at the iron bars of his cage. He could hear the sounds of prisoners shouting and banging things against their cell doors, desperate men struggling against the injustice of their reality. It had been two long days since guards had walked the white halls of the prison ward. Water was no longer running in the stainless toilets and faucets, and there hadn't been any delivery of food, toilet paper, or mail. Electricity had also been lost, making for some very dark nights in cells illuminated only by moonlight spilling in through small Plexiglas windows.

Having had plenty of time to watch TV before the crisis, Tanner knew good and well that the country had gone to pot. A virus was spreading faster than sightings of Elvis. Politicians had talked of freeing some of the prisoners in order to make it easier to care for those who remained. In Talladega, however, that plan had failed to materialize. Instead, the guard patrols became less frequent and then just stopped all together. It appeared that they had simply decided to let the prisoners rot in their cells.

Despite stories of poncho rafts and ropes woven from toilet paper, it was nearly impossible to break out of a medium security prison like Talladega's Federal Correctional Institution. Tanner's cell door was made from hardened steel bars that could not be cut or damaged with anything in his six-by-eight cell. He had but one hope, and that was that someone would let him out. Short of that happening, he would die. He understood this truth and waited as calmly as his nerves would permit. Remaining still not only allowed him to conserve his considerable strength but also to work on an inner peace that he had struggled with most of his life.

"In this world, people suffer," he said, reciting the first of the Buddhist Four Noble Truths. "This doesn't mean that I have to like it, only that I have to accept it."

After staring at the door most of the day, he began to doze off. Just as he was about to resign himself to being one day closer to his inevitable doom, he heard footsteps in the hallway. They were hurried and uneven, coming in quick shuffles followed by short pauses. He quickly got to his feet and moved to the door to look out. The man coming down the hall was wearing a blue guard's uniform, but his shirt was pulled out and unbuttoned, as if he had just stumbled out of a pub. As he got closer, Tanner recognized him as Ray Foster.

For a couple of years, Tanner had been teaching Kenpo Karate to Ray and three other guards. Not only did it lead to his receiving a few special perks from the guards, it also helped to keep his proficiency up, something that came in handy while in prison. Standing six-foot-four and weighing just over 250 pounds didn't hurt either. Even at fifty-four years old, Tanner was a tremendously powerful man by anyone's measure. Time, however, was every man's enemy, and serving a fifteen-year sentence all but ensured that his art would be lost if he didn't pass it on while in prison. The guards were quite receptive to being the student of a man who had proven the lethality of his style of self-defense on more than one occasion.

At this point, however, Ray did not look well. His face was swollen, his eyes were laced with bloody cobwebs, and his clothing was soaked in sweat. Even though Ray was as close to a friend as he had, Tanner stepped back from the jail cell door.

"What happened to you?"

"I'm no good," Ray mumbled, moving up to the bars and fumbling with a large ring of keys. "No good," he repeated.

When he found the right key, he held it up for Tanner to see.

"Only you," he said. "For what you did for me. No one else. Promise me."

Tanner said nothing.

"I cleared the entire lower ward yesterday. Only non-violents there. But here . . . ," he shook his head. "We can't let them out. Promise me."

"Okay, but they'll die. And not in a good way. Long and slow from dehydration."

"The lives they chose," he said, shrugging, before breaking into a long uncontrolled coughing fit.

When he finally recovered, he inserted a key into the door lock and turned it hard until a loud *clunk* sounded. The door moved inward a few inches with the weight of his body resting against it.

"Don't touch anything I touch," he said. "And don't get too close either."

Tanner nodded. No chance of that.

Ray turned and motioned for him to follow.

They made it as far as the prison courtyard before running into trouble. Ray was shuffling across the courtyard toward the prison's main gate, which was already propped open, when two men approached from the minimum security ward. One man carried a screwdriver and the other a three-foot length of pipe. From the twisted looks on their faces, they weren't out to offer thanks to the innkeeper for a comfortable stay.

"Hold up!" the man with the screwdriver shouted as he and his partner hurried to intercept them.

When Ray saw them, he started to run, but, after only a few steps, he fell. He struggled to stand back up but quickly lost his resolve and collapsed on the asphalt.

Tanner was deliberately ten or fifteen steps behind Ray, but it wasn't difficult to hustle into the path of the two oncoming men. Both were wearing orange jumpsuits identical to his, but he didn't recognize either man. When they came to within a few steps of Tanner, they stopped.

The convict with the screwdriver took a step forward, pointing it at Ray.

"He's got it coming. We got no beef with you, big man, but if you don't want some of the same, you'll step aside."

Tanner moved his right foot slightly behind his left, a position he had taken many times when confronting angry men.

"Let him be."

"They left us to rot in those cells, and for that, he's going to bleed."

"You look free enough."

"After two days of nothing to drink but my own piss."

"And here I thought that was just a milk mustache."

Screwdriver's cheeks turned a bright red, and he bit down hard on his lip.

"You think you're a funny man?"

"Don Knotts was a funny man. I'm something else."

"Two of us and one of you. That gives us the advantage," said Screwdriver. "Plus, we got weapons and you don't."

The man with the pipe tapped it against his palm to emphasize the point.

"Wrong on both counts," Tanner said, tightening his hands into fists the size of sledge hammers.

Ray moaned loudly, and all three men looked his way. Taking it as an opportunity to get the jump on Tanner, the first convict lunged forward with the screwdriver extended in front of him like a fencer might with an epee.

Tanner brushed it aside and leaned into a powerful ridge hand strike across the man's throat. The blow hit him with tremendous force, his head whipping back as his feet lifted six inches off the ground. He landed flat on his back with his head smacking the pavement with a wet *squish*.

The man with the pipe looked from Tanner, to his partner, and then back to Tanner. His eyes were wide with fear.

"Did . . . did you just kill him?"

Tanner nudged the fallen man with his shoe. He didn't move.

"Could be."

The man took a step back, dropped his pipe, and ran.

Early the next morning, Mason repeated his ritual of securing the cabin and loading his truck with supplies. He intended to return by nightfall but packed enough food and water to last a full week, in case things took a turn for the worse. He also secured the M4 assault rifle to a floor-mounted rack in the cab of his pickup. If trouble found him, he could have a long gun in his hands within a few seconds. He continued to carry Marshal Tucker's Supergrade on his hip, which he hoped one day to have the opportunity to return. Until then, he would use it for what it was intended. He was sure that Marshal Tucker would have wanted it that way.

As he pulled away from the cabin that had been such a big part of his childhood, Mason couldn't help but wonder if he would ever see it again. Nothing seemed certain anymore. What he did know was that it had saved his life by keeping him away from the virus, and, for that, he was thankful.

A little more than a mile down the road, Mason came upon the old blue pickup that he had discovered the day before. He pulled up beside it and stepped out. The inside of the windows were covered in a thick layer of black blowflies, the adult relatives of the hundreds of thousands of maggots that were busy devouring the bodies within.

Digging in his truck bed, he retrieved a few tools, two five-gallon gas cans, and a large roasting pan that he had brought from the cabin for one specific purpose. He lay down on his back and slid a few inches under the rear of the blue pickup.

The smooth shape of the truck's fuel tank was directly above him. He felt around until he found the flat drain cock at the base of the tank. Using a large flathead screwdriver, he pried the plug about halfway out. The fuel started to leak around the plug and onto his fingers. He quickly slid the pan under the drain to catch the gasoline.

When the pan was nearly full, he pushed the plug in enough to stop the flow and poured the fuel from the pan into the gas can. He repeated the procedure until the two gas cans were completely full. It worked, although by the time he finished, he had spilled as much gasoline on his clothes and the ground as he had transferred into the cans. He would need to figure out something more efficient later. For now, he had a simple method of keeping his vehicle fueled.

As he climbed back into his truck, Mason took one last look at the blue pickup. Thankfully, the three people within were spared from ever having to see the horror of the insect feast they had become. The world slowly took back all that it gave, and it was humbling to even the hardest of individuals to witness. He took a deep breath and turned his attention to the road.

❀ ❛

He saw his first signs of life less than three minutes later, as two men riding off-road motorcycles whipped around a sharp bend in the mountain road. They appeared so suddenly that he had to slam on the brakes and pull to one side to avoid hitting them. They sped past him, laughing and looking over their shoulders as they passed. Neither man was wearing a helmet, gloves, or any other motorcycle gear. Mason watched in the rear-view mirror to see if they would stop or continue on. After a few seconds, they motioned to one another and turned back in his direction.

Not wanting to get caught sitting in his truck, he opened the door and stepped out onto the unpaved mountain road. Mason made sure that his badge and gun were clearly visible on his waist. He had been in enough confrontations to know that running put you at a disadvantage that was hard to overcome. If these two were looking for trouble, he would give it to them head on.

The two men sped toward him, stopping when they got to within about twenty feet. They dismounted from the dirt bikes and walked in his direction slow and easy, like matadors approaching a *toro bravo*. Both wore dirty shirts, worn jeans, and work boots, none of which fit quite right. Neither man looked to have shaved or even taken a sponge bath in a couple of weeks.

The larger of the two looked as if he could have worked as a bouncer at an Irish pub, his plaid shirt filled out with tight muscles and his face covered in a thick red beard. He carried a hunting knife at his side that was canted forward for quick access. His partner was a full head shorter, with distinctly Asian facial features. He had two black teardrops tattooed below his right eye, and, more important, a Glock pistol sticking out from a makeshift holster on his waistband.

Mason nodded to them as they approached.

"Gentlemen," he said, keeping a watchful eye on their hands.

They nodded and advanced to within a few steps. He saw a sudden nervous look pass between them as they spotted his badge.

"Officer," Red Beard said in a tone that sounded well practiced.

"I'm a Deputy Marshal."

Red Beard smiled, his front teeth showing wide gaps between them as if he had used a woodworking rasp to floss.

"Close enough."

"What can I do for you men?"

"We were wondering if you might have any food or water," said Teardrops. "The folks in Boone were none too kind, and we're hungry enough to eat a horse, hooves and all."

"I'm out looking for supplies myself."

"There's nothing you can spare?" Teardrops glanced over at Mason's truck.

He shook his head.

"Sorry."

"You sure you're not holding out on us?" asked Red Beard.

Mason ignored the question.

"What can you tell me about Boone?"

Teardrops looked to Red Beard, and when he didn't answer, said, "Boone's the same as every other place we've been. Homes and cars are filled with rotting bodies. The stink is somethin' awful. It's almost like the dead rose up from their graves."

"Who's in charge down there?"

"Not the law if that's what you're asking. Close as we can tell, it's become a regular Wild West. People are killing one another for just about any reason." His eyes narrowed. "Even for food and water."

Mason nodded, thoughtfully.

"People do all kinds of stupid things. More often than not, it gets them killed."

Red Beard took a small step forward.

"I guess that makes you the Lone Ranger."

"You mean Wyatt Earp."

"Huh?"

"The Lone Ranger was a Texas Ranger. I'm a U.S. Marshal, like Wyatt Earp and Bat Masterson."

Red Beard looked irritated.

"My point was that you're all alone now."

Mason shrugged. "Do you know how many men Wyatt Earp killed?"

"What does that have—"

"Some say ten. Others bring the count all the way up to thirty. Can you imagine that? One man killing thirty. I'd wager there's a lesson in that somewhere."

"And what might that be?"

"I always took it to mean that a determined lawman will triumph over lowly cowards. Your takeaway might be a little different."

Red Beard's face tightened, and he squinted his eyes.

"I bet those same cowards eventually put him in the grave, though, didn't they, Marshal?"

"Not hardly. Wyatt Earp lived to the ripe old age of eighty. Now Bat Masterson—"

"Listen," said Red Beard raising his voice, "we don't give a hoot about what happened to your cowboy buddies. We need food and water."

"I thought we already covered that."

Teardrops said, "I guess we were hoping that after having time to get to know us, you might decide to share—"

"No."

A vein on Red Beard's forehead swelled, like a night crawler wriggling its way to the surface. "You're telling us that—"

"I'm telling you no."

Red Beard clenched his fists so tightly that Mason could hear the knuckles pop.

Teardrops reached over and patted his friend on the shoulder.

"It's no problem, Marshal. We're cool. We'll find something down the road a ways."

As Teardrops spoke, Red Beard slowly slid his hand toward the small of his back.

Mason squared himself, his gun hand hanging ready at his side.

"Just so we're clear," he said in a firm voice, "if either of you makes a move I don't like, I'll shoot you both."

Red Beard's hand froze, and he brought it back around front. Both men looked at each other, uncertainty in their eyes but a determined tightness to their jaws.

Teardrops took a step toward Mason, his hands spread open with the palms up.

"You got it all wrong, Marshal. We're not looking for any trouble."

Red Beard suddenly made a quick grab for the gun at the small of his back. Before the weapon could clear his belt, Mason drew the Supergrade and shot him twice below the throat. Both bullets punched through nearly the same hole. He immediately sidestepped and fired more two shots into the smaller man who was standing transfixed by the sudden explosion of violence. The first bullet passed through his heart, and the second split his sternum. Both men hit the ground at the same time.

Mason stood watching the wisps of burned gunpowder rise into the air, as if they were the spirits of the fallen men. He replayed every facet of the gunfight, including his draw, grip, trigger squeeze, and recoil control. Then, waking from the trance, he stepped forward and looked down at Teardrops. The vacant stare in his eyes told Mason all he needed to know.

He moved over and knelt down beside Red Beard. The man lay clutching his throat, like a prospector trying to hold back oil, blood pulsing out from between his fingers. He gurgled and coughed as he gasped for air, desperately trying to hang onto life. Mason reached out and placed a hand on his shoulder. Red Beard's eyes grew wide and tears began to stream down his face. He blinked once, then his body spasmed and he was gone. His big green eyes stared up at the sky like two polished emeralds floating in pools of milk.

Mason stood and looked down at the bodies. Only minutes before, these two men had been riding carefree through the mountains with the cold morning air stinging their faces. Now they lay dead, their warm blood slowly draining out onto the dirt beneath them. It had been a defining moment for them, one that they surely didn't appreciate the importance of until it was too late. Mason cleared his throat and spat. Such was life.

He carefully searched them, taking the hunting knife, the Glock pistol, and a small snub-nosed Colt revolver that Red Beard had been hiding behind his back. He put the knife on his belt and the two pistols into the glove box in his truck. Once he was certain they didn't have anything else that might be of use, he rolled the two bodies over the edge of the steep mountain road and kicked some dirt to cover the pools of blood. He walked the motorcycles off the road and leaned them behind a nearby tree. He would pick them up on his return trip. Mason didn't particularly enjoy riding motorcycles, but they were very fuel-efficient and might serve a valuable need if gasoline became scarce. From this point forward, it was all about survival.

As Mason continued his journey down to Highway 321, he couldn't help but replay his encounter with the two men. Both were surely convicts. The tattoo of the teardrops was common among those who spent time in prison. It occurred to him that many of the survivors of Superpox-99 might indeed be criminals. According to Jack, they had been released only after things had grown so dire that the nation's infrastructures were collapsing. Unlike the vast majority of law-abiding citizens who had been caught completely unprepared, the convicts would have had the chance to steer clear of others until the virus subsided.

As with shootings in his past, Mason couldn't help but wonder why he felt so calm after having just taken two lives. It wasn't that he necessarily expected to have regrets or second thoughts about his actions. Drawing down on the two men seemed justifiable in this new world where every man had to be held accountable for his actions. He was, however, surprised that he could control his body's unconscious processes, including his heartbeat and the release of adrenalin. Fellow marshals had accused him of having ice in his veins on more than one occasion. While that was meant as a compliment from one lawman to another, doctors had also warned that emotional baggage was like an audit from the taxman; while extremely unpleasant, it was something that eventually had to be dealt with.

Mason wasn't so sure. During his time in the Army's 75th Ranger Regiment, he had learned to kill without questioning why. The enemy was the enemy, nothing more. They had no children, no wives, no dreams for the future. They were simply the epitome of evil that had to be stopped. While such detachment might lead some to sociopathic behavior, it had enabled him to follow an internal compass that he believed always pointed true north. Life was easiest when viewed in black and white, right and wrong.

To force himself to stop rehashing things that were probably best left in the past, Mason began reviewing his goals for the excursion into Boone. Above all else, he needed to assess the scope and severity of the infection in his immediate area. Were the dead lining the streets as the convicts had suggested, or was there some semblance of society still functioning?

He had also compiled a list of supplies that he hoped to gather, not the least of which was additional food. He had a large stockpile of dehydrated and freeze-dried supplies in the cabin, but collecting extra canned and pre-packaged food was still prudent. Packaged products might last a year or two, and regular canned food could easily be safe to eat for five years.

Fuel was also a pressing need. Without adequate gasoline, he would be confined to the cabin, which would leave him isolated and potentially vulnerable. He had placed four empty jerry cans in the bed of his truck, two of which were now full. Using his method of draining fuel tanks enabled him to get around, but it relied on having frequent access to other vehicles. It also didn't account for the fact that fuel would eventually solidify into a gummy substance if it sat for too long. In a year or two, the gas in most of the vehicles would be unusable without some form of pretreatment. A fuel stabilizer was therefore high on his list of needs.

Next on his list were medical supplies. Mason had a fairly exhaustive first aid kit at the cabin, but he hoped to gather some broad-spectrum antibiotics, anti-diarrheals, and antiviral medicines, if any still existed. In addition to food, fuel, and medicine, he had identified a collection of miscellaneous items that might prove useful, including batteries, ammunition, matches, spare parts for his truck, toiletries, bottles of hand sanitizer, and disposable face masks. He had no idea if the last two items would in any way protect him from Superpox-99, but they seemed to be reasonable precautions to have on hand.

When he arrived at Highway 321, he paused once again to appreciate the scope of the devastation. Cars and trucks of every size and shape lined the four-lane divided highway. Some were smashed into one another; others had been driven off into the deep ravines lining the shoulder; a few were even propped up on the concrete divider, as if a huge bulldozer had plowed through the stalled traffic. This had been a scene of terrible suffering; people trying to escape something that was not escapable.

He turned east on the highway and began carefully navigating the congested thoroughfare. He spent much of the time driving on the shoulder, and more than once had to nudge a vehicle that was blocking his path. Most of the automobiles had bodies within, all now in advanced stages of decomposition. Even during his time in the wars in Afghanistan and Iraq, Mason had never seen so much death at one sitting.

After navigating through the blockade of vehicles for two long miles, he came upon a service station on the right side of the road. Attached on one side was a small convenience store and, on the other, a mechanic's shop that had been partially burned out. Two fuel pumps sat out front with an old rusty Dodge Charger smashed into one of them. A stamped sheet metal sign hung above the store, Sugar Grove One-Stop.

He pulled into the small parking lot next to the undamaged fuel pump. The pumps wouldn't operate without electricity, but they almost certainly contained fuel in their underground storage tanks. He waited in his vehicle for a full minute to see if anyone would come out to investigate. No one did.

Taking his M4 with him, Mason climbed out of his truck. He double-checked the chamber and slapped the magazine to make sure that it was fully seated. It was a safety click away from being ready for action. He positioned the single-point sling over his neck and shoulder so that the weapon could hang freely.

His first stop was the Charger that had crashed into the fuel pump. Thankfully, there were no rotting corpses inside. A few hand tools were scattered on the floor, and a small duffle bag was on the seat. He searched the bag and found only a set of women's clothes.

He left the tools and bag in the truck and walked to the front of the convenience store. The glass door was smashed, and several shelves that had been barricaded against it were pushed over into the store. A man lay face down on the floor a few feet inside. A .22 rifle was poking out from underneath his body, probably his last line of defense against looters. Hundreds of flies buzzed around his decaying corpse, taking their fill of the rotting flesh.

As Mason carefully maneuvered through the blocked doorway, the sour stink of decomposition hit him in the face like a sweaty boxing glove. He forced himself to take shallow breaths through his mouth as he proceeded into the store. Most of it had been thoroughly ransacked. The shelves were tipped over and the glass cooler cases smashed. Candy, chips, bottled drinks, and a mishmash of food products covered the floor. If not for the dead body, it would have been a junk food paradise.

"U.S. Marshal," he called out. "Anyone alive in here?"

For several seconds, there was no reply. Then he heard a faint scratching sound coming from the back of the building. He brought his M4 to the ready and slowly approached the small hallway at the rear of the store. On one side were the men's and women's bathrooms, and on the other was a storeroom. He stood in the hallway and listened. The scratching sounded again, clearly coming from the storeroom.

Standing to one side of the door, he bumped on it with the muzzle of his rifle.

"This is Marshal Raines. Anyone in there?"

The only answer was the same scratching sound.

He tried the door knob, but it was locked from the inside.

"Stand aside," he said. "I'm coming in."

Mason lined up with the door and gave it a good kick. The frame split and the door swung in. Inside was a young woman sitting at a small table. Based on the advanced stage of decomposition, she had been dead for more than week. A large pool of blood, organs, and bile had spilled across her chair and onto the floor. Much of her flesh was split, and several bones were already visible.

Lying beside her chair was the largest dog Mason had ever seen. Covered in a thick coat of gray, brown, and white fur, the Irish wolfhound rested just outside the pool of the woman's blood. The dog didn't look long for this world.

"Hey, boy. You okay?"

The dog winced and scratched the floor. His eyes were only half-open, and his huge tongue hung from his mouth like a wet mop.

Mason approached the dog slowly and squatted down. It made no effort to get up. He wondered if it had contracted the virus. The woman in the chair had blisters covering her arms and face, but he saw no signs of blisters on the dog's skin. Mason knew that most viruses didn't cross-infect between species, but he couldn't be sure if that was true of Superpox-99.

He knelt beside the dog for nearly a minute, considering his options. The smart thing to do would be to walk away, perhaps putting a bullet in the dog to end its suffering. Before he could firmly make up his mind, the dog slid its head forward to rest on the toe of Mason's boot.

"I hear you," he said, reaching down and petting the animal's head. "You're not ready to give up just yet."

The dog whined.

"I don't suppose you can stand?"

It looked up at him with two different-colored eyes, one blue and the other brown.

"That's what I figured," he said, scooping up the huge animal into his arms. The dog offered no resistance, not even a growl. Instead, it draped over the sides of his arms like a sleeping child being carried to bed.

Mason couldn't believe how heavy the dog was. Even suffering from dehydration and malnutrition, it easily weighed over a hundred pounds. He carried it from the convenience store out to his truck and placed it on the tail gate. Then he opened the passenger-side door.

"If I let you ride up front, you're going to have to promise not to puke up anything. Deal?"

The dog blinked in response.

He scooped the dog up again and placed it on the seat.

"Stay here while I get you something to eat and drink." There was no point in breaking into the supplies in the back of his truck when there was a store full of them only a few steps away.

He re-entered the store and searched through the debris. On the floor, he found several unopened bottles of water and a tray full of miniature cans of cat food. He dumped out a couple of three-liter bottles of soda and used his newfound hunting knife to cut the bottoms off to act as makeshift bowls.

As he exited the store, supplies in hand, Mason heard the distant sounds of traffic approaching from the east. He sprinted back to the truck, tossed the supplies on the floorboard, and slid into the driver's seat. Being caught with very little cover and only a lame dog to back him up was not his idea of a solid defensive position. Seeing no other option, he quickly pulled the truck around to the back of the convenience store. There was nothing large enough to hide it behind, so he parked it as close to the building as possible.

As he stepped from the truck, the dog gave a soft *woof*.

Mason looked over at him. The dog struggled to raise its head.

"You've got more courage than strength. Let me handle this. You rest."

The dog slowly lowered its head and closed its eyes.

Mason readied his M4 and went to the corner of the building to see who was approaching.

A caravan of four RVs and two campers traveled single file down the highway. One camper rode at the front and one at the rear, running sentry for the convoy. When they neared the service station, the vehicles slowed to a stop.

The door to the lead RV opened, and two men and a woman stepped out. The men were armed with rifles, and the woman carried a pump shotgun. She stayed by the RV while the two men went up and checked out the store. After a couple of minutes, they returned. One of the men had his arms full of snacks, and the other carried their rifles.

Mason decided to take a chance. He swung the M4 to his back and shouted from the corner of the building.

"Hello there!" he called, waving his hands.

They all turned in his direction. The man carrying the snacks quickly dropped them to the ground, and everyone raised their rifles. However, no one took careful aim. Mason took a step away from the building, ready to dive for cover if needed. The three talked among themselves and then turned back to him and waved.

"Hello!" one of the men yelled.

Mason took that to be a good sign. Careful to keep his hands where they could see them, he walked toward the group. When he got to within a few yards, he stopped. The three kept their weapons in hand but didn't point them directly at him. Another good sign. They didn't know it, but they were in just as much danger as he was. Mason could draw and shoot all three in just over one second, faster than most people could even comprehend a situation, let alone react.

The two men were in their late forties or early fifties. The woman was perhaps a few years younger. All looked exhausted. The older of the men stepped forward and offered his hand. Mason shook it.

"Good to see a friendly face," the man said. "I'm Carl Tipton, and this is my brother, John, and his wife, Jules." The others nodded and smiled at Mason.

"I'm Mason Raines."

Carl looked down and saw the badge on Mason's belt.

"Well, I'll be darned. I haven't seen one of you Marshals since my days as a bail bondsman."

"I don't suppose you've encountered other law enforcement officers?"

"Not a single one. Of course, there are plenty of cop cars littering the streets. But I can't say as I've seen anyone alive in uniform." He looked to John and Jules. They both shook their heads.

"Most of them abandoned their posts when things got bad," said Jules. "Who can blame them? Family comes first for all of us." To emphasize the point, she reached out and placed a hand on her husband's arm.

"Have you been through Boone?"

All three stiffened at his question.

"Yes sir, we have," answered Carl. "I wouldn't advise you go that way, especially with that badge."

"Why's that?"

"The place has been overrun by a gang of thugs. Not what you'd call law-abiding citizens. The worst part is that I suspect there are quite a few survivors hiding out, just too afraid to come out of their homes for fear of being victimized."

Mason nodded, giving his words the attention they deserved.

"Sounds as if somebody's going to have to go into Boone and help those folks."

Carl sighed. "I suppose you're right. But that would be a tall order. You'd probably have to put down more than a few people in the process."

"Did you folks run into any trouble?"

"Nothing we couldn't handle," he answered, glancing over at John. "There are sixteen armed adults in our convoy. The old adage about there being strength in numbers apparently holds true when society falls apart."

The RV door opened, and the face of a young girl peeked out.

Jules looked up at her and said, "It's all right, Lucy. This man's a U.S. Marshal. He's a good guy."

Wearing a pair of wrinkled capri pants and a bright yellow shirt, the girl descended the stairs. She smiled and gave a short little wave.

"Hi."

"Marshal Raines, this is our daughter, Lucy."

"Pleased to meet you, Lucy," Mason said, returning her smile.

"She's the bravest ten-year-old in the entire world."

"I bet she is."

"Mom," said Lucy, obviously embarrassed.

"It's true," said John. "When this all started happening, Lucy was a real trouper. Never cried, not even once."

"You couldn't say the same about me," Jules said with a nervous laugh.

John put his hand on her back. "We're all dealing with the impossible."

"Marshal Raines, will you be coming with us?"

"Great idea, Lucy." Carl turned to Mason. "We could really use a man like you."

"It would sure make me feel safer," added Jules.

Mason rubbed the stubble on his chin, thinking about their offer.

"Where exactly are you folks headed?"

"West toward Johnson City and Kingsport, wherever there might be folks setting back up. Truth is we may be on the road for a while."

Mason smiled and shook his head.

"I appreciate the invitation. I really do. But I'm not quite ready to move on just yet. Who knows? Maybe we'll meet up sometime later."

Only Lucy seemed surprised by his answer.

"Understood," Carl said, looking around and surveying the service station. "Mind if we help ourselves to a little gas before we move on?"

Mason thought about the two dead bodies inside the building.

"No one here would care," he said. "Take what you need. I'll probably fill a couple cans myself."

"Many thanks," said Carl, motioning for Jules and her husband to get the refueling supplies.

Mason followed them to the circular refueling ports located on the ground a few paces away from the pumps. There were four ports, each topped with a different-colored lid.

When Carl saw Mason looking over his shoulder, he said, "The red, white, and blue covers are all different grades of gasoline. The big plus symbol on top indicates that the fuel is unleaded. The yellow one here is diesel. That's what we need most right now."

Carl and John used a pry bar to remove the yellow cover. Beneath it was a large cap with a protruding handle. John knelt down and removed the cap. Underneath was a six-inch diameter pipe leading down into an underground fuel tank. Jules lowered a rubber hose into the pipe. The other end was connected to a small pump with a battery-powered hand drill attached. A matching hose, attached to the pump's output port, was routed into a large gas can. When everything was in place, Carl activated the drill, and fuel began pumping from the tank into the can.

"That's handy," Mason said, thinking how his method of fuel retrieval paled in comparison.

"John rigged that up for us," Jules said with a proud smile. "It's simple, but simple is good when everything's falling down around you."

After watching for a couple of minutes, Mason said, "I'm going to check on a friend. I'll be back in a few."

Carl nodded, not taking his eyes off the drill pump system.

Mason walked around to the back of the building. The dog was still in the same condition as when he had left. He poured some bottled water into one of the makeshift bowls and dumped some cat food into the other. He set them on the seat and lifted the animal's head so that it could eat and drink. It didn't take long for the dog to start lapping up the water. When it had drained a full bowl, it turned its attention to the cat food. It quickly finished two of the small cans before laying its head back down on the seat.

"All right, let's see if you can keep that down," Mason said, petting him on the back of his neck. The dog stared up at him, obviously enjoying the attention.

"You're going to need a name."

The dog looked at Mason intently, its ears folded back.

"You're big, that's for sure. And determined to stay alive. Plus you've got those two mismatched eyes, as if your body couldn't decide which one to choose. Hmm . . . What shall it be? Twinkles?"

The dog stared at him without any reaction.

"No? Grizzly then?"

Again, nothing.

Mason thought for a moment.

"I've got it. I'm going to call you Bowie."

The dog tipped its head sideways.

"It's perfect. There's Jim Bowie, the famous frontiersman and hero of the Alamo, and there's David Bowie, the musician with two different eyes. Not sure if they're different colors, but that's close enough. Sound good?"

The dog set its head back down and licked the seat to see if any cat food might have spilled out.

Mason patted the big mutt on its side.

"I can't promise things are going to get any easier for you, Bowie. But fate brought us together, so let's see what else she has in store for us."

& &

After saying goodbye to Carl, Jules, and John, Mason spent the next few hours carefully searching the convenience store and burned-out automotive repair shop. He loaded up several plastic crates from the back of the store with an assortment of snacks, cigarettes, batteries, toiletries, and over-the-counter medications, all of which could be useful, or, at the very least, traded as barter goods.

In the garage, he found a large rack of car and truck parts, several cases of motor oil, four brand new Diehard batteries, a couple more empty fuel cans, and a red metal chest filled with hand tools. His greatest find, however, was a two-kilowatt inverter. The unit, which was about the size of a thick briefcase, would enable him to convert DC battery power into AC power. It even had an adapter that allowed it to be plugged directly into a car's cigarette lighter. While two kilowatts wasn't a great deal of power, it was enough to power a microwave oven, a computer, or nearly any other small electronic item with a standard three-prong plug.

When Mason came across an automobile fuel pump and some rubber tubing, he decided to try to build a fuel retrieval system similar to the one that Carl had demonstrated. He started by securing the fuel pump to a small piece of plywood using metal straps and wood screws. Next, he attached a ten-foot length of tubing to the input and output ports. For power, he wired the pump's terminals to one of the car batteries using an electrical switch that he took out of the partially burned wall.

He carried the apparatus over to the fuel ports that Carl had explained earlier and lowered the input hose down into the underground tank of unleaded fuel. He put the other hose into one of his gas cans and turned on the pump. The unit sputtered briefly as air was purged from the system, but then it began to pump out gas in a smooth, powerful stream. Mason couldn't help but grin at his accomplishment. As long as reserves were available, either underground or in vehicles, his fuel problem was essentially solved. He continued running the system until he filled up the remaining fuel cans and topped off his truck.

As Mason loaded the fuel retrieval system into the truck bed, Bowie sat up and leaned his head out the passenger side window.

"You're feeling better."

Bowie laid his head on the windowsill as if to argue the point.

"I said better, not perfect, you big baby."

Bowie looked at him and yawned.

"I've got a load full of supplies, and you're going to need some time to recuperate. I had hoped to push into Boone today, but I think we're better off returning to the cabin for a couple of days." After what he had heard about Boone, it didn't seem wise to roll into town with darkness only a few hours away.

He fed Bowie another can of cat food and then began the six-mile trek back to the cabin. Traveling the roadway was a little easier because Carl and his caravan of RVs and campers had cleared a decent path. The biggest risk was running over broken glass, tail lights, and other debris that might puncture a tire. Mason had a spare tire secured under the bed of the truck, but he had no desire to use it.

As he approached Buckeye Road, the turnoff from Highway 321, Mason saw a car approaching from the opposite direction. It was an older model Impala, and the driver didn't seem to be in a hurry. As the Impala came to within a few car lengths of Mason's truck, it slowed and stopped. Mason had already unlatched the M4 and was prepared to take cover behind his truck if things took a turn for the worse.

A heavyset man stepped from the Impala and waved to Mason.

Bowie sat up and peered over the dash. The dog's ears were standing straight up as it stared intently at the stranger.

Mason rolled Bowie's window all the way down.

"If I get into trouble, I expect you to remember who fed you."

The dog's only response was to look at him and then back to the stranger.

Leaving the M4 in its rack, Mason exited the truck and walked slowly toward the man. Unlike his previous encounter with Teardrops and Red Beard, this man appeared quite harmless. He was a portly fellow, balding except for puffs of white hair along his temples, and dressed in a blood-stained priest's vestment. If he had been holding a shepherd's crook, the man could easily have passed for Friar Tuck.

"Good morning," he said with a friendly smile. "I'm Father Paul." He didn't offer a handshake or a last name.

"Marshal Raines."

"I seem to be having better luck today."

"Oh? Why's that?"

"Not more than two hours ago, I met several families traveling westward. Now I'm talking to a peace officer. Good luck indeed."

Mason figured that the families that he was referring to must be Carl and his caravan of RVs.

"Are you on your own, Father?"

"Never truly alone," he said, gesturing up to the sky. "And yourself?"

Mason thought of his missing family and friends. He shrugged.

"For now."

"It seems we are two men in uniform with little more than our sense of duty."

"I suppose so."

"Are you coming from Boone?"

"No, I didn't get past Sugar Grove. What about you? Are you headed into town?"

"Oh, yes. I live there. I was away visiting sick friends in Elizabethon when this all happened. I stayed on after their passing to help the good people there. I've done what I can. It's in the Lord's hands now."

"From what I've seen, He has his hands plenty full."

"It's the end of times, my friend. One would expect the Lord to be busy."

"No offense intended, Father, but if it's the end of times, shouldn't you have been called up into heaven? Revelations and all that?"

The priest smiled and rubbed his chin.

"I must confess that I've wondered about that myself. I can only assume that the Lord left a few of the faithful behind to do His will. I feel quite honored actually, as should you."

"Me?"

"Of course. Nothing happens purely by chance. You are here for a reason no less important than my own."

"Fair enough. I suppose we'll each do our part, whatever that may be."

The priest leaned in close like he was about to share a secret with an old friend.

"My part will be to heal the sick, bless the dead, and help feed the hungry. What will yours be, Marshal?"

Mason didn't respond for a moment, but the priest stood patiently awaiting his answer.

Finally, he said, "I suppose I'll stand in the way of those who would do harm. It's what I do."

Father Paul bowed his head slightly.

"A peacekeeper. God surely has need of such men in these troubled times. May He bless you on your mission of justice as He does me on my mission of mercy."

"Amen to that," Mason said, wondering what his "mission of justice" might ultimately require.

CHAPTER
9

Ray Foster didn't get back up. Tanner tried to coax him to his feet from a safe distance, but the man just waived him on.

"Go," he breathed. "Just go."

There seemed no reason to argue the point, so he left Ray lying in the prison yard. How long he would live, Tanner couldn't say. But he suspected it wouldn't be long.

He walked out the front gate of the prison, a slave who had suddenly awoke to discover that he had been emancipated. The weather was comfortable, and his orange jumpsuit was enough to keep away the chill. Not having anywhere else to go, Tanner walked east along Renfroe Road in the direction of a large plume of black and gray smoke. Whatever was on fire had plenty of gas and oil to keep it going.

After walking about a half mile, he came upon a site more appropriate to the streets of Mogadishu than eastern Alabama. A UH-60 Blackhawk helicopter had crashed into the roof of a Church's Chicken fast-food restaurant. Bright yellow flames licked out from the wreckage, although the blaze was clearly on the way to burning itself out. The building was in pretty good shape, from the outside at least. Soot-colored smoke billowed between the small row of restaurants and shops, as if an old Indian medicine man was enjoying his favorite pipe of kinnikinnick.

The two intersecting roads were deserted save for a few cars that had either been abandoned or become the final resting places of their owners. The small community was as quiet as a graveyard, not a single soul standing around gawking at the most unusual sight.

A young girl, perhaps ten or twelve years of age, stumbled to the edge of the roof, doubled over and coughing. She was standing dangerously close to the edge, obviously trying to escape the heat of the fire. Tanner watched to see if anyone else would appear on the roof. No one did.

The girl looked up and saw him. She started motioning frantically for his help. He hurried across the street and stood next to the brick wall of the restaurant. She was about ten feet above him, teetering on the edge of the roof.

"Help me," she cried, coughing.

He looked around but didn't see anything that could easily be moved to lift him up. Seeing no other option, he said, "Hang off the edge and drop. I'll try to catch you."

"I can't. It's too far."

"Suit yourself," he said, turning to leave.

"Wait! What are you doing?"

He turned back.

"If you want my help getting down, you'll have to hang and drop."

"Are you sure you can catch me?"

Tanner shrugged. "I don't know. I've never caught a girl falling from a burning building. But I'd say the odds are better than fifty-fifty."

From the disappointed look on her face, she apparently didn't appreciate his honesty.

"Okay, okay," she said, first sitting down and then sliding her legs over the edge.

He moved close to the building and reached up. She was still about five feet out of his reach.

"Okay, now lower and drop."

She carefully lowered herself, but as she was about halfway down, she started to cough, lost her grip, and fell backward.

Tanner saw her fall but accepted that there wasn't much he could do to change what would happen next. He moved back half a step and spread his arms as wide as possible, hoping to act as a human net. The girl landed butt first on his left shoulder and then fell backward as if tumbling off a teeter-totter. He managed to cross his arms around her ankles, just in time to prevent her from flipping completely over his shoulder. When she finally stopped falling, she lay dangling across his back with her feet up near his head.

Tanner carried her across the street and set her on the curb. The girl's whole body was trembling.

"Relax," he said. "You're okay."

She nodded. "But it was close."

"Yes, it was close."

"You did good. Thanks."

He smiled. "How old are you, kid?"

"I'm eleven," she said, stiffening. "I'm just short for my age."

He sized her up. "No, I'd say you're about right for eleven."

"You look . . . well, you're as big as Oscar."

"Who's Oscar?"

She looked back toward the helicopter.

"He was my bodyguard. He's dead now."

"What kind of kid needs a bodyguard?"

She shrugged.

"That's not much of an answer. You got rich parents or something?"

"Something like that."

Tanner looked back at the wreckage.

"Where were you headed?"

"To my mother's."

"Where's she at?"

"Virginia. It's east of here."

"I know where Virginia is."

"Any chance . . . you're headed that way?"

"I'm not really headed anywhere."

"You just break out of jail?"

She pointed to his orange jumpsuit, which had the word "prisoner" stamped across the front and back.

Tanner looked down at her and furrowed his brows.

"For your information, I was released."

She nodded slowly, obviously not buying the story.

"Okay. Does that mean you don't plan to kill me?"

"I don't *plan* to."

"Okay," she repeated.

They both turned as they heard several loud motorcycles approaching from the north.

"Come on," he said. "Let's get off the street." He turned and hurried over to a small submarine sandwich shop with a sign above it that read, Vinny's.

The girl stared up the road, weighing whether the motorcycle riders might prove more helpful than a reluctant rescuer wearing a prison jumpsuit. After a few seconds, she turned and followed him.

A handwritten sign hung on the window informing would-be patrons that the restaurant was closed until further notice. Tanner tried the door, and wasn't surprised to find it locked. He bumped it with his shoulder, and the lock broke free of the doorjamb.

"Come on," he said, ushering her in and pushing the door closed behind them.

A few seconds later, a group of four men rode into the intersection. Tanner recognized one of them as Wesley, a fellow inmate who had been doing time for molesting his neighbor's fifteen-year-old babysitter. Like most sexual predators, he tended to stay with his own type while in prison. Wesley was a big man known in the yard for two things: he was the only inmate capable of bench pressing more than five hundred pounds, and he enjoyed forcing himself on young men who were new to prison.

For the moment, the four riders seemed completely enthralled with the helicopter crash. Tanner didn't know how long that was going to last, but he was sure that, if they found the girl, she would become the unwilling object of their affection.

He turned to her. "Look around for somewhere to hide."

"Okay," she said, her face turning a sickly shade of white.

She walked around the small store, opening cabinet doors and looking in closets.

After a brief search, she said, "I found something."

When Tanner turned around, he saw that she was holding a large revolver with both hands.

"It was under the cash register."

"Bring it here."

She held it out in front of her like a pair of dirty work boots. When she got close, she suddenly had a change of heart. "Maybe I should keep it with me."

"There's only one problem with that."

"What?"

"That's a Taurus Judge."

"So?"

"It's loaded with .410 shotgun shells, which means it will kick like a stick of dynamite. Even if you could pull the trigger, which I doubt, it would jump right out of your hand or, worse, smack you in the forehead."

"Oh." She handed it to him.

He opened the cylinder and saw that two of the five shot shells had already been fired.

"What's your name?" she asked.

"I'm Tanner. You?"

"Samantha. You can call me Sam, if you want."

"Okay, Sam. Have you found a place to hide?"

"Under the sink, maybe. But if they look, they'll find me."

"I'll give them a reason not to look. You stay put until I come back or you hear them drive away. Got it?"

"Yes."

As he opened the door to leave, she said, "For what it matters, I hope they don't kill you."

❧ ❦

All of the men had dismounted from their bikes and were standing around watching the helicopter burn. By the time Wesley saw Tanner approaching, they were only a few car lengths apart. Tanner had stuck the Judge in the front of his waistband where it would be clearly visible. Big as Wesley was, he wouldn't want to take a .410 load to the chest.

"My man Tanner," Wesley said in a voice loud enough to draw everyone's attention from the rooftop spectacle.

Tanner nodded to him. "Wesley."

"I didn't know they let you out. I thought you hard timers were going to end up food for the rats."

Tanner moved to within a few feet of the group.

"Most of them are still locked up."

"You get out for good behavior?" he said, making a vulgar motion with his hand.

Tanner didn't answer.

"You should get rid of those scrubs. Someone's gonna to take a shot at you."

Tanner saw that Wesley was wearing jeans, a pullover, and a black leather jacket. All of the clothes looked brand new. The other three men were similarly dressed in new biker clothing.

"Where'd you get the duds?"

Wesley pointed up Highway 275.

"We found a Harley Davidson store just up the road. An old guy was hiding inside, but he didn't mind us taking what we wanted."

"He definitely didn't mind," added one of the men, laughing.

Tanner wouldn't be baited into hearing about their violence.

"You ever seen anything like that?" he asked, gesturing to the helicopter.

"Nope," answered Wesley. "Looks military to me. Did you check it out?"

"Still too hot. Even if it wasn't, it looks all burned out."

Wesley nodded, looking around.

"You see any survivors?"

Tanner shook his head.

"I doubt anyone could've walked away from that."

"It doesn't matter anyway. It's a brave new world, my friend. And we're gonna be the conquerors. You should come with us. Fun times ahead, I promise you."

"Thanks, but I think I'll go my own way." Tanner turned to walk away.

Before he had even taken two steps, Wesley spoke.

"You know I always wondered . . ."

From his tone, Tanner knew there was going to be trouble. He looked back over his shoulder, his hand instinctively sliding up to the grip of the Judge.

"Yeah?"

"I always wondered if you were really as tough as everyone claimed."

The other three men stood up straight, their eyes glazing over with cruel intentions.

Tanner pulled the Judge free, spun around and fired three times. With each boom of the cannon, a man fell. When the smoke cleared, only Wesley remained. His hand gripped a Beretta pistol stuck in his waistband, but he was so shocked by what had happened that he had yet to pull it free.

"Toss it," Tanner said, pointing the empty Judge at his chest.

"Why did you go and do that?" Wesley said, his voice a mix of anger and disbelief.

"This world doesn't need any more conquerors. Now, toss the piece, slow and easy."

Wesley pulled the pistol out and tossed it about ten feet away.

"Now what?"

Tanner threw the Judge over by Wesley's Beretta.

"Now, I answer your question."

It took Wesley a moment to understand the situation. When he finally did, his lips curled up into a confident smile.

"So, that's how it's gonna be?"

"Yep."

Without hesitating, Wesley charged him like a linebacker looking for the game-winning sack. Tanner managed to deflect much of Wesley's energy by spinning away to his right and landing a solid elbow to his ear. If it had been a few inches further back, he might have dropped the big man with a single blow to his mastoid.

As it was, he ruptured Wesley's eardrum and sent him stumbling away. Tanner immediately stepped forward and shot a front kick at Wesley's knee. The kick contacted with a muffled crunching sound, and his leg bent to the side as ligaments tore free. Wesley screamed in pain and lunged for Tanner again. This time, he managed to get both arms high around his waist.

Tanner was a big man, but Wesley was an ogre. Not only was he giant, he was also incredibly strong. Using his superior strength to his advantage, he pulled Tanner into a bear hug, pinning one of his arms against his body. Wesley's knee wouldn't quite keep him upright, so he stayed bent over as he applied the powerful hold. Tanner felt his ribs compressing as if he had been caught in a junkyard car crusher. He felt around with his trapped hand and found the inside of Wesley's thigh. Grabbing a handful of the tender skin, he tried to rip it away. Wesley screamed and shifted his body.

Tanner felt a weakening of the bear hug and tried to break free by jerking violently to one side. Just as Wesley's fingers came apart, Tanner leaned in and dropped a powerful elbow onto the back of his neck.

Wesley fell to his weak knee, stunned by the blow. Tanner grabbed the back of his head and drove his knee up into the man's face . . . once, twice, three times.

Wesley fell back unconscious, his nose broken and his eye socket partially crushed. Bright red blood drizzled from his nose, and his eye bulged out like an overripe cranberry. Wesley wouldn't be a threat to anyone for quite some time. Tanner started to walk away, and then thought better of it. He turned back and, with a powerful stomp to the head, snapped Wesley's neck.

憄 憖

Samantha said, "I saw what you did out there."

"I figured."

"Were they bad men?"

"Yes."

"That's why you killed them?"

Tanner thought about it a moment.

"Could be."

"You don't know why you killed them?"

He sighed. "We have to go."

"Where?"

"You said you wanted to head east."

"So you're going to take me?"

"You'd rather I leave you here?"

"No."

"Then, I guess I'll take you."

"All the way to Virginia?"

Tanner shrugged. "Let's take it an hour at a time. You talk a lot."

She didn't say anything for a few seconds, pressing her lips tightly together.

"Proving me wrong?"

She grinned.

"I can tell this is going to be a long trip," he said, shaking his head.

"I should warn you that my mom says I'm socially awkward."

"What exactly does that mean?"

"I think it means that I don't always say the right things."

"Who does."

"We're going to need food and water for the trip."

Tanner pointed to a large glass case filled with bottled beverages.

"We'll need other things, too. Backpacks, blankets, and flashlights. I've been camping a few times, so I know about these things."

"I think we can find most of what we need in the stores around here."

"What about a car?"

He looked out the window.

"Plenty to choose from. You got a preference?"

She thought for a moment.

"Something red?"

"Fine. You stay here and see what food and water you can round up. I'll go get some clothes and a car."

"Where are you going to find clothes big enough to fit you?"

Tanner thought of Wesley's new biker clothes.

"I'll find something."

President Glass couldn't stop crying. Tears rolled down her makeup like beads of rain across the surface of a waxed limousine. The president's bedroom was deep underground, and she felt as if she was living in a cave at the center of the Earth. It was her personal hiding spot, similar to the closet that a child might retreat to when afraid. And, like that child, President Glass was deeply afraid.

Her worst fears had materialized. The country had died. The world had died. Her husband had died. Her daughter was missing and presumed dead after her helicopter reportedly crashed. Nothing remained for President Glass. She didn't know why she had been spared. She didn't want to be spared. Not now. Not in the lonely hell that remained.

A small chirp sounded from the secure phone on her nightstand. Conventional phone service had been lost all across the country, but engineers had managed to wire up the emergency operations center in Bluemont, Virginia, to satellite communications.

She rolled over and put the pillow over her head.

The phone sounded again.

She wanted to ignore it. Answering it meant making decisions, and that was something she felt utterly incapable of doing. If she had her way, they would just let her wither away like flowers on a grave.

The phone continued to ring.

She sighed and picked it up.

"What?"

"Madam President, are you feeling better?" The voice was that of Lincoln Pike, her newly appointed vice president. The elected vice president had died from the virus two weeks ago. As the Speaker of the House, Lincoln had all but insisted that he be appointed vice president. With few other options available, she had finally acquiesced.

"I'm sleeping. What do you want, Lincoln?"

"I think we should meet."

"Why?"

"There are matters to attend to, Madam President. Serious matters."

She wanted to argue the point, but she knew he was right. The country needed leadership now more than ever. Unfortunately, she was not up to being that leader.

"Fine," she said. "When?"

"Tomorrow. I've already arranged a flight."

"Tomorrow isn't good."

He hesitated, choosing his words carefully. When he finally spoke, his voice was soft and warm.

"Allow me to help you, Madam President."

She wiped tears from her eyes and swallowed hard. Lincoln cared about her in the way a lion cared about a wounded gazelle. She considered refusing to see him. But then what? He would be relentless until he got his way.

"Fine. Tomorrow at noon." She hung up the phone and fell back into bed.

৵ ৶

There was a strong knock at Vice President Pike's door.

"Enter."

The door opened and General Hood stepped inside. With his perfectly pressed uniform, cluster of commendation medals, and spit-shined shoes, he looked every part the professional soldier.

"Have a seat, General."

"I prefer to stand."

The vice president smiled. He liked General Hood. He was smart, ruthless, and most important, trustworthy.

"What did you find out?"

"The girl was not at the crash site."

The vice president pushed his chair back from the desk.

"How's that possible?"

"It appears that she survived and fled the scene."

"With who? Surely not alone."

"Unknown, sir. There appears to have been a firefight. Four men dead."

"Killed with military weapons?"

"No, sir. Three were killed with a shotgun. One was beaten to death."

"That sounds more like a street fight, probably involving some of the miscreants that the president felt compelled to release from our penal institutions."

"It would seem so."

"You know, whoever grabbed her might just solve this problem for us."

"I prefer to clean up my own messes."

The vice president nodded.

"I assume you're actively looking for her."

"Yes, sir. We have two helicopters in the area. A small ground contingent is also en route, but they won't arrive for some time."

"Do you think she'll try to make contact with friendly forces?"

"Assuming that she's able, that would be a logical course of action."

"Find her before that happens."

"Yes, sir."

"The man I have leading this effort can be trusted implicitly. He will do exactly as we instruct. You should also use only your most trusted people. There can be no leaks on this, General."

"While I would trust the soldiers with my life in combat, this mission is unconventional. Some may have to be expunged when the operation is complete."

"Expunged?"

"Yes, sir."

The vice president nodded again.

"We do what we must to save this struggling nation."

"Indeed," said General Hood. "I do wonder, however, if it might be prudent to inform the president of the girl's possible survival."

"Why?" The vice president's eyes narrowed with suspicion.

"If we get to the girl first, then the plan remains unchanged. However, if she turns up elsewhere, such a report might help to deflect suspicion."

"Ah, yes, I see your point. The problem is that, if the president even suspects that the girl is alive, she will use every possible resource to find her. We can't have that. Certainly not now when we're so close."

"Understood."

"For now, let's allow her to assume the worst. It helps to keep her weak and ineffective, and that's the only way we can save this nation from the coming evil."

తొ 札

The tray of food looked like something from a hospital cafeteria. President Glass picked at a blob of green gelatin as if it was an alien life form. As a child, she had always liked Jell-O. In her current state, however, she saw it as a food perversion that was hard to look at, let alone eat. A knock sounded on her office door.

"Enter," she said with as much authority as she could muster.

Vice President Pike entered. He nodded and offered a smile.

"Madam President."

She looked down at the food before finally pushing it aside.

"Lincoln."

"Thank you for agreeing to see me. I know you must be very busy."

She squinted at him. Was he digging at her? Of course he was.

"Yes, I am. So, let's make it quick."

"Yes, of course," he said, sliding out a chair. "Right to the point, then. Madam President, we have a very important decision to make."

"And that is?"

"As you know, the virus claimed about ninety-five percent of our population. Of the roughly twenty million people remaining, it's estimated that nearly five million were exposed to the virus, but subsequently survived."

She closed her eyes, wondering how her own family could be counted in the dead.

"I'm familiar with the numbers. What are you getting at?"

"Madam President, it may be even worse than we thought."

She fought back tears.

"Nothing could be worse."

He slid his chair a little closer.

"Ma'am, I've been told by several CDC scientists that they are seeing an unexpected side effect of the virus. One that could threaten the remaining population."

"What kind of side effect?"

"They describe it as acute delusional paranoia."

"Paranoia? Like believing people are out to get them?"

"Yes, but it's very specific. Those affected seem to target their paranoia toward people who were not exposed to the virus."

"They probably just feel like outcasts, that's all. Have you seen what the virus has done to these poor souls? Besides, how could a virus cause paranoia?"

"It appears that Superpox-99 introduces chemical changes in the brain. Those changes cause the person to feel overwhelming paranoia. It continues to deepen over time, until they eventually lose touch with reality."

She shook her head. "Even if that's true, it doesn't necessarily threaten the population. You're reaching here, Lincoln."

"I'm sorry, ma'am. I'm not making myself clear. In time, the paranoia leads to horrible violent tendencies. Those who are most strongly affected become consumed with an overwhelming desire to kill."

"Let me get this straight. You're saying that the people who survived the virus are going to try to murder the people who weren't infected?"

"Yes ma'am, it appears so. Not all at once, of course. Each person reacts differently, but on the whole, it's . . . well, it's quite serious. Before long, we'll have a nation that is heavily infested with *crazies*, for lack of a better term."

President Glass closed her eyes and sighed.

"Can't we administer some form of cure for this madness?"

"No, ma'am. There aren't enough resources left to develop such a medicine, assuming that it could even be made."

"So, what then? We just let what's left of our country be overrun by millions of violent, mentally deranged . . . whatever the hell they are?"

The vice president moved even closer, hoping to circumvent any microphones that might be in the room.

"We will need to take action to prevent this."

"And what do you propose?" She didn't see where he was going but was certain she wasn't going to like it.

"I think we need to sort our population into those who were infected and those who were not. That way, we can keep them apart from one another, at least until we can develop a treatment for this disorder."

President Glass looked at him as if he had just grown antenna.

"You're proposing we set up internment camps?"

"I wasn't planning on using that term. But to be blunt, yes, ma'am, that's exactly what I'm proposing."

"To what end? What if we don't find a cure to the paranoia? What then? Do we keep millions of Americans in camps until they die? What about their children? Are they suspect, too? Where does this end, Lincoln?"

He sat back in his chair, considering her words.

"I see your point, Madam President."

She smiled, finally feeling that she had gotten the better of a man she despised, if for no other reason than for his unshaken confidence.

"Yes, yes, you're absolutely right," he continued. "I see it now. The internment camps would never work."

"Thank you," she said. "I'm glad that—"

"There really is only one solution."

"And what's that?"

"We have to finish what the virus couldn't."

Mason spent the entire next day at his cabin. Not only did it give Bowie time to rehydrate and regain his strength, it also gave Mason time to connect with others on the ham radio. He talked at length with several people around the country. It seemed that things were essentially the same everywhere—people were dead, and structured society had all but disintegrated. The hardest hit areas were urban centers, where people lived in close proximity. By all reports, big cities were places of pure horror, the likes of which even the most gruesome zombie movies couldn't portray.

By mid-afternoon, he began picking up an official government radio broadcast. The message was transmitted on numerous shortwave frequencies and repeated every few hours. It started with the familiar Emergency Alert System tone, followed by a robotic voice issuing a simple announcement:

Due the outbreak of the Superpox-99 virus, the nation's utilities have been disrupted. Citizens are encouraged to shelter in place for thirty days, or until the virus has subsided in their area. The nation's government remains committed to safeguarding the public. Distribution of critical supplies, including food, water, and medicine will begin soon. Until that time, survivors are urged to band together to ensure their survival.

In one sense, it was good news. It meant that some portion of the government was still functioning. On the other hand, it was as grave an announcement as the federal government would ever issue. It also seemed highly unlikely that they would be distributing supplies anytime soon, given the unprecedented loss of life. It was much more likely that the government currently had little, if any, control of the country.

He assumed that the recommendation to shelter in place for thirty days was meant to give the virus time to kill off those who had already been infected. The problem was that most people had less than a week's worth of food on hand and no stockpile of clean water. Broadcast or not, necessity would drive people to seek out essential supplies.

Later in the day, Kate and Jack also signed on as had been previously agreed.

"It's good to hear your voices," said Jack.

"For me, too," agreed Kate.

"Does anyone have a pressing announcement?"

"I'm assuming that you've both heard the government's broadcast advising people to shelter in place," said Jack.

"Good advice but a bit late," said Mason.

"Do either of you believe what they said about food and water being distributed soon?" Kate sounded much better than when they had previously spoken.

"Not a chance," said Jack.

"It seems like a stretch to me as well," said Mason.

"That's what I figured."

"I have been picking up rumors that the government is re-establishing at the outskirts of several large cities," said Jack. "I heard Denver mentioned in particular."

"That's good, right?" asked Kate. "If the government gets up and going, they'll eventually provide some relief to those of us who survived. They have to; it's their responsibility."

Mason wasn't so sure. The nation was passing through uncharted waters. What would happen next was anyone's guess.

"Kate, my advice is not to depend on the government or anyone else coming to your aid. Given the size of the devastation, help is going to be very slow in coming, if it comes at all. Do either of you have an idea of the number of dead?"

Jack was quick to answer.

"I've been asking around, but no one knows for sure. Based on my small survey, and it's definitely not scientific, I'd say that maybe one person out of every twenty or thirty is still alive. Some contracted and survived the virus. As you can imagine, they're pretty messed up. Others of us just stayed away from it. And, finally, it seems that a few, including Kate and her son, were just flat out immune."

"My God," said Kate. "Can that be right? Could there really be hundreds of millions of Americans dead?"

"If you push those numbers to a global scale," said Mason, "we're talking about many billions."

"Take my estimates for what they're worth. All I know for sure is what I see around me. The streets are littered with cars. Homes are quiet because no one is alive inside. Bodies are everywhere. That's my reality. Are you two seeing something different?"

"I haven't been into any towns or cities yet, but I can confirm that the streets are as you say. Very few people alive here," Mason said, thinking briefly of the encounters he had during his last outing.

"I try not to go out much," said Kate. "But, yes, you're right. Almost everyone is dead around me. I do occasionally see a car go by on the road behind my house, but not more than once or twice a day. I haven't had the courage to approach anyone."

Mason said, "Kate, you're sheltering in place just as you should be. When things right themselves and it's time to seek help, you'll know it. For now, keep yourself and your boy safe."

"I'm not sure that I can continue to do that."

"Why's that?" asked Jack.

"My big need now is gasoline. I took the gas cans from my neighbors' garages, but I'm almost out. Without gas, I won't be able to run the generator, and, without the generator, I won't be able to use the radio or anything else requiring electricity."

"Cars are all around you with fuel in their tanks. You just need to pump it out."

"How do I do that?" she asked. "With a siphon?"

"As long as the gas can is lower than the gas tank, the siphon will work fine," replied Jack. "The problem is that most cars have anti-siphon blocks. That makes it a bit tricky to get the hose down into the tank. Are you good with your hands?"

"Uh, no. It took me nearly half a day to figure out how to drain my water heater."

Jack was slow in answering.

"Marshal, you got any ideas?"

"Kate, you should be able to retrieve fuel just like you did the water."

"Tell me." Her voice sounded hopeful.

"You'll need to drain the fuel tanks of the cars in your neighborhood. If you look underneath a vehicle, you'll see a large container located toward the rear. If you see hoses running out of it, you can disconnect or cut the lowest hose and drain the tank that way. If you can't access the hoses, look for a flat drain plug on the very bottom of the tank. The drain cock can be pried out with a flathead screwdriver. If all else fails, use a sharp screwdriver and a hammer to puncture the tank at the lowest point. You'll obviously need to be ready with a container that can be slid beneath the car and still hold a lot of liquid."

She thought for a moment.

"Would a child's swimming pool work?"

"Better than a roasting pan," he said, laughing.

"I'm sorry, what, Marshal?"

"I said it sounds perfect."

"I can't thank you enough. Please don't give up on me. I'll get stronger and more capable. I promise."

"Kate, I'm not going to give up on you. You and Jack are the closest things I have to friends in this entire world."

᷁ ᷁

A deep rumble, like that of a large boat propeller sputtering through choppy waves, sounded from far away. Mason pushed it from his mind, dropping down once again into the dark abyss. Something wet touched his ear, and his eyes shot open.

Bowie bumped him again with his giant nose. Mason sat up, straining to see through the darkness. Bowie turned to face the bedroom door, his growl growing louder and more menacing.

Mason reached down and put his hand on the dog.

"Shh," he said.

The dog quieted, but the growl still rumbled deep in its chest.

Mason slid off the bed and grabbed his Supergrade from the nightstand. He approached the bedroom door, walking lightly on the balls of his feet. Bowie followed closely beside him, his claws clicking against the aged wooden floorboards. Mason paused and listened at the door. For several seconds, he heard nothing. Then, just as he thought Bowie had disturbed his sleep for nothing, there was a loud metallic clang that sounded like a large spoon falling off the counter.

Mason told himself that it was probably just raccoons. He reached for the doorknob, but stayed his hand before turning it. He listened and waited.

A sharp whisper sounded from the cabin's main room.

"Quiet!"

Bowie turned to him as if to ask if he had heard it, too.

Mason patted him and nodded.

The door to the bedroom was made from two-inch thick, solid oak planks, more than enough to stop a pistol bullet or even shotgun pellets. A high-power rifle or shotgun slug might get through, but not without first losing much of its punch. As with most doors, however, the lock itself could easily be destroyed. Fortunately, in his experience, intruders tended to ignore locks and shoot for the center of doors instead.

Mason considered his options. He could take cover in the bedroom. Even if they managed to breach the door, he would have a decent chance at pegging them in the doorway. The problem was that if he didn't take them all out quickly, they'd use the walls of the cabin as cover, making for a prolonged gunfight. With only nine rounds in his Supergrade and no spare magazines in the bedroom, that scenario didn't bode particularly well for him.

Option two was to slip out the bedroom window and hide out in the tree line until they left or he could initiate a successful attack. The risk there would be that they might hear the heavy window slide open and try to intercept him around back. Also, there was the problem of leaving Bowie to fend for himself, something he was not prepared to do. Taking the dog with him wasn't possible either because, even in his wildest dreams, he couldn't imagine Bowie fitting through the small window.

His mind made up, Mason quickly slipped on a pair of blue jeans, a black tee shirt, and his boots. He also secured his pistol in its holster, and double-checked the knife on his hip. He squatted down beside the dog.

"I need you to make some noise."

Bowie stared at him and then turned back to look at the door.

"That's right," he said. "Good boy. But wait until I'm ready."

The dog turned back to the door, its ears standing straight up.

Mason moved to the window, unlatched it, and gave it a light tug upward. As he suspected, it was stuck. He looked back at Bowie.

"Okay, boy, get 'em!" He raised his voice with the last two words, and Bowie got the message. He charged to the door and began barking wildly.

Mason jerked the window upward, and thankfully, it came free. The cool air spilled into the room like icy water into a submerged vehicle. He wasted no time, leaning out the window and falling forward. He hit the ground, rolled on one shoulder, and quickly scrambled to his feet. It wouldn't have earned him many points in a gymnastics competition, but it did get him out and ready to fight very quickly.

Mason ran around the cabin while keeping close to the wall to avoid setting off the flood lights. When he came to the front, he hopped over the railing onto the porch and peeked around the corner. Not fifteen feet from

him was a man standing at the top of the stairs. He was holding an assault rifle at the ready, but his back was to Mason.

A man with long dreadlocks charged out the cabin door, looking back the way he had come. The two men exchanged words, and the man with the rifle shoved him back toward the cabin. Dreadlocks reluctantly re-entered, pistol in hand.

The man outside the cabin brought the rifle to his shoulder and watched intently at what was happening inside. Mason drew his knife and held it low, at the ready. Staying in the shadows for as long as possible, he charged across the porch.

By the time the man saw Mason approaching, it was too late. He barreled into him, sending both of them down the stairs to slam into a large red Hummer that was parked out front. They bounced off the truck and fell to the ground.

Landing on top, Mason thrust the knife up under the man's rib cage. When it hit his backbone, he jerked it out and stabbed again. With the second blow, the man immediately grew limp, his arms falling away to his sides. Leaving the knife sticking out of him, Mason snatched up the rifle and rolled onto his back to face the cabin door. The door to the cabin was still open, but no one came out to check on the commotion.

Taking a moment to examine the rifle, he saw that it was a cheap, Chinese-made AK-47, not something he was willing to let his life depend on. He tossed it aside and drew his Supergrade—not as much firepower but much more reliable. He waited another ten seconds, but no one came out of the cabin. Seeking a better fighting position, Mason stood and quietly advanced to one side of the door.

From inside, he heard Dreadlocks say, "That damn bedroom door must be a foot thick. I don't care what Ricky says. We're not getting through it without a grenade."

"Let's just take what we can and get the hell out of here," said a second man. "I got a bad feeling about this place."

"Ricky thinks there might be a woman hiding in there. Remember how sweet that peach was from the Zippy Mart."

Both men laughed, the unmistakable sound of lust in their voices.

"You know that Ricky will take her first," said the second man. "He'll probably hurt her a bit, too."

"Long as she's still kicking, I'll get mine."

Both men laughed again.

Mason leaned around the doorframe just far enough to peer into the cabin. Dreadlocks was standing with his back toward Mason. The other man was facing him, but his view was mostly blocked by his partner. Both were carrying handguns and flashlights. The man further away was wearing either a down vest or some form of body armor.

With just his hand and part of his face exposed, Mason raised the Supergrade and shot Dreadlocks in the hamstring. As Dreadlocks fell, the second man raised his pistol and blindly fired two rounds in Mason's direction. One bullet splintered the top of the doorframe, and the other passed through the open doorway. Mason shot him twice in the groin and once through the left eye. He fell back against a small table, draping over it like a dirty rug.

Dreadlocks screamed in agony, clutching his leg and rolling around on the floor. He still had his pistol in one hand, but his flashlight had fallen away.

"Throw the gun away," Mason ordered, taking aim at him.

Dreadlocks rolled to his side to see who had shot him. He started to raise his pistol but decided against it.

"Okay, okay. I'm throwing it," he moaned. He tossed the gun several feet away. "Don't shoot me again."

Keeping his pistol aimed at Dreadlocks, Mason stepped into the cabin. A shape suddenly rushed past him from outside. The giant creature descended on the prone man, tearing into him with horrible ferocity. Mason instinctively jumped back and raised his weapon. Only then did he see that it was Bowie.

He moved to grab the dog, but stopped when he realized there was no point. Dreadlocks was already dead, his throat torn out with one powerful rip from Bowie's massive jaws. Mason stood back, watching as the huge dog shook the man from side to side like he might a child's doll. When Bowie was satisfied that the man was dead, he dropped the lifeless body to the floor. He turned back to look at Mason, the fur around his mouth wet with blood.

Mason gestured for Bowie to come to him, and the dog immediately obeyed. He bent over and patted Bowie on his side.

"That's a good boy." There could be no mixed messages. When it was time to fight, it was time to fight. "All I want to know is how you fit through that window."

Bowie looked up at him and licked the blood off his lips.

Mason rolled the last body off the bed of his truck, watching as it tumbled down the steep mountain pass like an out-of-control skier. It settled several hundred feet below, not too far from the bodies of the other two men he had killed on the roadway. He rolled up the plastic sheeting that lined the bed into a tight bundle and secured it with a length of black paracord. He suspected that it might come in handy again one day.

He sat down on the edge of his tailgate, and Bowie immediately flopped down beside him, taking up nearly half of the truck bed. With all three men dead, Mason had no way of knowing how they had found his cabin, where they were from, or whether they were part of a larger group. His best guess was that they had come from Boone, since it was the closest town, but it was nothing more than a guess. What was clear was that they were bad guys out doing bad things, and that was enough for him.

He reached down and scratched the dog's thick neck.

"We got lucky this time."

Bowie's hind leg bounced up and down with excitement from each scratch.

"From here on out, we're going to need to be more careful. Let's start by making the cabin a bit less accessible. We can drag a few dead trees across the driveway and make the turnoff a bit harder to see by obscuring it with brush. Also, I'll start parking the truck around back. That will help some, but the truth is we need to think about securing more than just the cabin."

Bowie raised his head and watched as squirrel ran up a nearby tree. When he was satisfied that it was outside his reach, he flopped back down on Mason's lap. Unlike his newfound master, he didn't have a care in the world.

"We could turn this place into a fortress and try to ride things out until the government gets back on its feet," Mason continued. "A good defense is sometimes enough, yes?"

Bowie looked up at him and gave a short *woof.*

While it sounded logical, Mason wasn't entirely convinced. For one thing, the condition of the government was unclear. Some officials had almost certainly been sequestered in time. The broadcasts seemed to confirm as much. But when and how they would emerge to take charge was anyone's guess. The lack of broadcasts on the police scanner suggested that law and order had broken down, at least in his immediate area. People were operating in survival mode with every person out for himself. The stability that had taken hundreds of years for the country to establish was destroyed in a few short weeks.

The good news was that people were still alive; the human race hadn't been wiped out. Decimated perhaps, but not exterminated. There were still people like Carl, Jules, and Father Paul, who were out there working to ensure that mankind would carry on. It made sense for Mason to do his part as well. He needed to help systematically establish the rule of law. That might be a tall feat, given the current demographics, but it was nonetheless necessary.

Boone seemed a reasonable place to start. It sat too close to his cabin to allow it to remain lawless and violent. It would only be a matter of time before another group of men stumbled onto his retreat and either cleared it out while he was away, or, worse, cut his throat while he was asleep. Cleaning up Boone was an important step to ensuring his own security.

Once Boone was safe, Mason could turn his attention to bigger challenges, including checking on his father in Talladega's correctional facility and his mother in New York. He could also try to get word to the Marshal Training Center in Glynco that he was able to assist, assuming there was anyone there who even cared. Or anyone there at all.

CHAPTER
12

Mason understood that his mission in Boone would require more than a single lawman riding in and doling out justice like he was at the O.K. Corral. He hoped to start with a quiet, unobtrusive survey of the situation. People who survived the pandemic would be frightened. Rolling in and haphazardly shooting lawbreakers on sight would only make matters worse.

Before the outbreak, there had been roughly seventeen thousand people living in Boone. If Jack's estimate was anywhere near correct, Mason might expect to find a thousand people still alive. Hopefully, that would be enough to establish a viable society that could sustain itself until the larger government got up and going. If not, they would suffer the same fate as many of the early settlers, the vast majority of which starved or died of disease.

For the third time in less than a week, Mason spent the morning loading his truck with supplies. Once again, there was no guarantee that he would make it back to the cabin in a timely manner, so he packed plenty of extras, including food, water, fuel, and ammunition.

He also added a double-magazine pouch to his belt. With eight rounds in each spare magazine and nine in his Supergrade, that would hopefully be enough for him to fight his way to his rifle. He loaded five magazines for the M4, each with thirty steel-tipped 5.56 mm rounds. While Mason had always been more proficient with a pistol than a rifle, he nevertheless appreciated that rifles put out far more firepower, and at longer ranges. He had told his students many times that the primary purpose of any pistol was to help them fight their way to a rifle or shotgun.

When Mason got everything loaded and ready, he and Bowie set out on their trip to Boone. They drove all the way to Sugar Grove without encountering a single traveler. When he arrived at the convenience store where he had found Bowie, Mason spotted a white Toyota Corolla sitting in front of the fuel pumps. The driver's side door was open, and a body was lying on the asphalt a few feet away.

He slowed to get a better look. The corpse was that of a young man who couldn't have been much older than twenty. His skull and face had been crushed, and the ridged impressions from a framing hammer were clearly visible on the bone. The man's arms and legs were sticking out at awkward angles, stiff with rigor mortis.

Mason stopped the truck, grabbed his rifle, and stepped out. He motioned for Bowie to follow. The dog immediately began smelling the ground, making its way to the Corolla. Mason followed, keeping an eye on the convenience store. The car's backseat was filled with supplies—bags of cereal, jugs of water, blankets, and an assortment of clothing. The passenger seat had a yellow sweater draped across the back. There were two open bottles of water in the cup holders, along with a large open bag of beef jerky sitting on the center console. Whatever had happened to these people, it had occurred with little warning.

Mason walked around the front of the car and felt the hood. It was cold. He turned to Bowie, who had his snout buried in the bag of jerky.

"Hey."

Bowie looked up at him, a piece of beef jerky sticking out of his mouth.

"Stay here and watch the truck."

Bowie took a quick look around, and, when he was satisfied they weren't in any danger, turned his attention back to the food.

Mason walked around the outside of the building looking for signs of what had happened to the missing woman. He didn't find any. His best guess was that she might have been taken by the three men who had invaded his cabin the previous night. There was no way to know whether she was still alive, but, based on what he had overheard, it didn't seem likely. He did a quick search of the store, but she wasn't inside either.

Mason didn't want to leave when someone might need his help, but he resigned himself to the fact that he couldn't possibly right all the wrongs of the new world. He returned to his truck and whistled for Bowie. The dog came running, although, at its size, it looked more like a horse galloping in the derby. Bowie scrambled up into the cab of the truck as if fearing he might get left behind.

They pulled out of the service station and back onto Highway 321. Mason glanced in his rearview mirror to take one final look at the abandoned car and dead body. He suspected that it wouldn't be the last time he would feel a sense of helplessness.

Highway 321 changed names and became King Street at the edge of Boone. As were the other roads, King Street was cluttered with cars, many of which had been pushed to the shoulders and up onto sidewalks to allow a single lane of traffic to pass. Some of the cars were empty, but many were filled with swarms of blowflies that buzzed about like evil shadows trying to find a way out into the world. Both sides of the street were lined with a variety of shops that had once sold sporting goods, books, ice cream, and souvenirs. Mason had always found Boone to be a quaint place with the kind of charm only found in small towns that had a longstanding history behind them. In this case, the history revolved around the life of Daniel Boone.

The street was not entirely deserted. A few people were searching through stores and cars, undoubtedly looking for supplies. Fortunately, no one seemed particularly dangerous. Mason wasn't sure what he had been expecting, perhaps a cross between Dodge City and Fallujah. As it turned out, there was no overt violence anywhere. Not at the moment anyway. People were just out trying to meet their basic needs by good old-fashioned scavenging.

Having been through Boone several times before, he knew that the town was only about three miles across. Much of it directly or indirectly supported the Appalachian State University and the Appalachian Regional Medical Center. He suspected that the medical center in particular might be useful. While he doubted that the hospital was still operating, there might at least be a valuable assortment of medicines and supplies, assuming they hadn't already been pilfered.

At the center of downtown was the Church of the Fallen Saints, a historical landmark that was over one-hundred-and-twenty years old. Mason had passed it at least a couple of dozen times in the past but had never gone inside. As he approached the church, he wasn't surprised to see Father Paul's Impala parked out front.

Mason drove his truck up over the curb and onto the grass directly in front of the church. He and Bowie got out and surveyed the area. A woman and a young boy were across the street watching them with obvious concern. Mason waved. The woman put her arms around the boy, and they quickly ducked into the closest store. So much for small-town hospitality.

Turning to the church, he gave the massive oak door a push. Despite its size, the door swung open with surprisingly little effort. Bowie pushed his way in and Mason followed. Things were not as he had expected. The smell of human decomposition was nearly overpowering, causing him to retch from the stink. While there were only a few bodies within sight, the floors and pews were covered in dried blood and cadaver island stains, which resulted from the release of fluids during decomposition. A lot of people had died in this building.

Mason grabbed a hymnal and propped the front door open—anything to get a little fresh air circulating.

An excited voice sounded from deep inside the church.

"Marshal Raines!"

Mason turned to see Father Paul hustling toward him. He was wearing a black union suit and elbow-length rubber gloves covered in blood and hair.

"Good to see you, Father," said Mason, his voice sounding a little nasal as he forced himself to breathe through only his mouth.

"And you, my friend." Father Paul worked off the long gloves and draped them over a nearby pew. "I had a feeling that you and I might cross paths again."

"It's funny you should say that. I felt that way as well."

"I am often reminded that all things are connected like the strands of a spider web."

"Careful. You sound a lot like my dad, and he's a devout Buddhist."

"Do you know the difference between a Buddhist and a Catholic?" the priest asked with a warm smile.

"No."

"Nor do I. Whether we call it God's divine plan or the world's oneness, the results are the same."

Mason nodded, looking around the church.

"I hate to be the one to tell you, but you'll never get the smell of death out of this place."

"And yet, we try in all things."

"Indeed we do. In fact, that's why I came to Boone."

Having checked out the ground floor, Bowie suddenly appeared from around the corner of a pew. Father Paul immediately backed away, mumbling some sort of prayer to act as a protective incantation.

Mason said, "It's all right, Father. Bowie is a friend."

The priest stopped retreating but couldn't take his eyes off the dog.

"That animal is a beast of war if I've ever seen one."

Bowie approached the priest, slowly and cautiously, obviously sensing the man's fear. When he got close enough, he hopped up on his hind legs and placed his front paws on the priest's shoulders. The dog's head was a good six inches higher than Father Paul's.

The priest let out a shriek. He stopped when Bowie lowered his head and licked the man's face with his huge tongue.

"What in the world?" exclaimed the priest, wiping globs of slobber from his cheek. "How can a creature be so fearsome and yet filled with so much love?"

"He's just trying to find his way in this new world. A world in which violence and love are both needed."

Bowie nuzzled his snout against Father Paul's neck and whined. The priest reluctantly put his arms around the beast and gave him an awkward pat. Bowie dropped back to the floor, circled the priest one time, and returned to stand beside Mason.

Father Paul approached and put his hand on Mason's shoulder. "My friend, I think you came to see me for a reason. How can I be of assistance?"

Mason was still struggling to breathe with the awful stench and motioned for the priest to follow him to the open doorway.

"I'd like to help the people of Boone get back on their feet. Specifically, I want to help them put in place a rule of law that is followed and enforced."

Father Paul rubbed his chin in thought.

"To do that, we would first need to ensure that basic necessities are met. Without food and water, people will do what they must to survive. Unfortunately, that has meant taking things from others, sometimes at the point of a gun."

"Then we'll start by setting up the necessary infrastructures."

"Besides the violence motivated by necessity, we also have a serious problem with a large gang of criminals."

"Convicts?"

"That would be my guess. They certainly weren't here before this crisis."

"Do you know how many?"

"Thirty or forty, I'd guess. I've heard that their leader goes by the nickname of Rommel. Taken, I suppose, from the famous general in World War II."

Mason rolled his eyes.

"Criminals and their nicknames."

"He's reputed to be particularly ruthless, but what else would you expect."

"Then I'll start with him. My experience is that, if you cut the head off the snake, it dies rather quickly."

"True, but these are hard men," warned Father Paul. "None are going to cower at the sight of a single lawman."

"I've dealt with hard men most of my life."

Father Paul smiled a sad smile.

"I believe you. And I also believe that you are exactly what this town needs. Why else would God have brought you to us?"

"And here I thought it was my idea."

The priest patted him affectionately.

"He works through each of us in different ways, but always with gentle nudges. The choices are ours to make."

"Fair enough."

"How do you plan to deal with these criminals?"

"I'll start by kicking the hornet's nest and see what happens. In the end, blood will almost certainly be spilled. I want you to understand that going in."

"The hand of righteousness must sometimes be called to strike down evil. I have no illusions about that."

"I've found that violence is never far behind me. The same has always been true for my father as well."

"Oh, is he a lawman too?"

Mason thought a moment before shaking his head.

"No, but I suppose he could have been. He's as tough as nails to be sure. Unfortunately, he's also an angry man, and that ultimately landed him behind bars. Given the president's initiative, I'm not sure if he managed to find his way out of prison, or . . . if he didn't."

"I'm sorry. I pray that he finds his way to peace, wherever he might be."

"I'm sure he would appreciate that."

Father Paul clapped his hands together.

"There's much work to be done. Are you willing to lend a hand?"

"I am. I wondered if we might start by calling the townspeople together. Perhaps even bring them here?"

"That's an excellent idea. The Lord's house is always an appropriate venue to bring hope to those who are suffering."

"Do you have any idea how we can get the word out?"

Father Paul thought for a moment, and then a big smile came over his face.

"Follow me."

The sound of church bells rang out over the town of Boone like the song of angels over a bloody battlefield. At first, people merely stared in the direction of the church, uncertain of what it could mean. Then, a few at a time, they came. Christians and atheists alike gathered their loved ones and sought solace in their community's oldest establishment. Some were motivated by simple curiosity, most by faith and hope.

After three hours of incessant ringing, the entire church was filled to capacity. There were easily three hundred people in the building and another hundred outside leaning in to listen through doors and opened windows. Those who gathered spanned every demographic element: old and young, mothers and fathers, wealthy and poor, black and white. They looked tired, dirty, and afraid, but they also shared an excitement, like miners who'd been freed from an underground grave.

Even before Father Paul got up to speak, the huge room was buzzing with activity. People hugged, talked, and cried. When he finally walked up on the dais and raised his hands in the air, the priest looked like the ringmaster at a traveling circus.

"Brothers and sisters," he said, "may I have your attention, please?"

The room slowly fell silent.

"For those of you who don't know me, I'm Father Paul."

Several people clapped and shouted words of encouragement.

He smiled and gestured to them.

"Let me begin by saying thank you for coming. Whether you are a Catholic, Protestant, Jew, or atheist, no one can doubt that we are living in a time unlike any before. If ever there was a moment to gather in fellowship, it is now."

One man shouted, "Christ is coming!"

Father Paul smiled. "He is indeed. Whether that is now or later, no man knows. What I do know is that the town of Boone, and indeed the rest of the world, is suffering."

Several people said, "Amen."

"You are probably wondering why I have called you here. The truth is that I need your help." He held his hands out before him as he had done countless times before when asking people fill the church baskets with their tithing.

The huge mass of people fell silent, waiting for his request. Waiting to see if any of this even mattered.

"Our town is filled with unspeakable horrors—bodies lying in the streets, cars and homes filled with death and decay. Violence at every turn."

A woman started to sob loudly, mumbling something about her late husband.

"But we are still here," continued Father Paul. "Many have died, but we did not. God chose us to be here."

More amens filled the room.

"Don't ask me why, because I don't know why. All I know is that we are being called upon for a nearly impossible task—to rebuild our families, to rebuild our town, to rebuild our nation!"

A long round of applause sounded.

When it quieted, he continued.

"God wouldn't have left us here without the tools and resources that we need to survive. We must, therefore, set aside our fears and rise to His challenge. Indeed, there will be sacrifice and suffering. But there will also be joy and victory."

A man stood up near the front of the church.

"Father, will the government help us rebuild? We can't do it on our own."

"Perhaps one day, but, for now, we are most assuredly on our own. We must work together to establish our infrastructures: food, water, and electricity. Even more important, we must regain the trust of our neighbors and learn once again to depend on one another. God is reminding us that we are all brothers and sisters. It's time we listened."

People clapped for nearly a full minute.

"We can do this!" one man yelled.

A beautiful woman with thick, black hair and naturally tan skin stood up from the middle of the church. She was wearing medical scrubs.

"We must also provide at least some basic level of medical care. People are suffering from dehydration and infection. We can't afford to lose any more. Each life is more precious than ever."

"I couldn't have said it better," said Father Paul. "Miss, are you a medical doctor?"

"Yes," she answered. "I'm Avany Moura. I worked at the ER center."

"Dr. Moura, we are delighted to have you here," Father Paul said, nodding his head to her.

"Please, call me Ava. The time for titles and other formalities has long passed."

"Indeed." He turned back to the audience. "Do we have any other doctors here?"

An old man near the back of the room stood.

"I specialize in cardiac care."

Another man pushed in through the door.

"I'm an obstetrician."

Ava said, "I know of two other doctors and several nurses who also survived. We've been treating the sick and injured at the hospital. It's not much, but we're doing what we can."

"God bless you for that," said Father Paul.

"What about the gangs?" a woman shouted from the back of the church. "We'll never be safe with them roaming the streets. They killed a young man in front of my children yesterday."

Several people shouted their agreement, and the room became chaotic as everyone started talking among themselves.

Father Paul raised his arms again.

"Your attention, please."

The talking continued but in more hushed tones.

"Yes, we must deal with the violence," he continued.

"How?" the same woman shouted. "No offense, Father, but sharing God's word isn't going to work with these thugs."

"No," said Father Paul, "such men are not easily convinced to change their ways. That is why I have asked Marshal Raines to help us." He motioned for Mason to come up on stage.

When Mason and Bowie moved up beside Father Paul, the entire room came alive. Everyone seemed more concerned by the giant dog than comforted by the marshal's presence.

Mason leaned over to Bowie and said, "Announce yourself."

Bowie looked at him, and then back at the large audience. When Mason continued to stare at him, the dog finally let out a loud *woof!*

A few people in the front row shifted in their seats, looking around anxiously for a way out of the packed church. Nearly everyone fell silent.

Mason grinned. "That's Bowie, and I'm Deputy Marshal Raines. We're here to help you take back your town."

A heavyset man shouted, "How you gonna do that, Marshal? One man and a dog ain't near enough."

"We don't want no trouble!" yelled a black woman from the back of the church.

"If you make them angry, they'll kill us all for sure," said an older lady sitting, in the front row.

Ava stood up again, and Mason found his gaze drawn to her. She met his eyes and spoke.

"Marshal, people are afraid that you will somehow make things worse."

"I understand," he replied. "There's no question that there's a choice to be made. The townspeople of Boone can hide in the shadows and hope that these thugs will eventually tire of raping and killing—"

Several people started to grumble at his words. Ava grinned, never breaking eye contact.

"Or," he said, raising his voice, "they can push back and tell these men that nothing will come easy. That, for every life they take, the town will demand two."

"An eye for an eye," said the old woman in the front row, nodding. "That's God's way."

"Call it what you want," said Mason, "an enemy does not become more of an enemy when you fight him."

"Will you help us to fight them?" Ava asked, her voice soft, as if it were just the two of them sharing a private conversation.

"Yes, I will fight them."

"And you're good at that?"

"I am."

She nodded and sat back down.

A man with his arm in a sling struggled to his feet.

"Marshal, no disrespect, but there are dozens of criminals. Even you and that beast can't possibly stand up to all of them."

"That's true," Mason said, reaching down and petting Bowie. "Even with a friend like Bowie, I can't triumph over forty men. Are there others here with experience in law enforcement who would be willing to stand with me?"

Mason stood quietly, looking at the townspeople, wondering if anyone would find their courage. After nearly a minute of silence, a man in his sixties stood up in the front row. His wife was tugging at him to sit back down.

"I'm Max Blue. I was the police chief here in Boone until I retired a few years back. I'm not as fleet of foot anymore, but I can help."

A man wearing a sidearm got to his feet.

"I'm Vince Tripp. I was a Watauga County Deputy Sheriff, and I'll stand with you, Marshal."

A third man, fit and muscular but balancing on a prosthetic leg, rose.

"Don Potts. I spent four years as an MP in the army. And, if you don't mind this," he said, patting his leg, "I'll fight at your side."

Finally, a wiry man wearing an old plaid shirt, dirty blue jeans, and a straw hat stood.

"My friends call me Coon on account of I've been known to eat one on occasion."

Several people snickered.

"I don't have any law enforcement experience to speak of, but I can hit a squirrel in the nuts at a hundred yards. If you need shootin' done, I'm your man."

Mason nodded. These brave misfits would be his deputies.

Executive Order 16661

Establishment of the Viral Defense Corps

By virtue of the authority vested in me by the Congress, and as the elected President of the United States, the following is hereby ordered:

Section 1. Establishment of the Viral Defense Corps. An agency shall be established in the Department of Defense that shall be known as the Viral Defense Corps (VDC). The VDC shall be headed by the vice president until a permanent director can be appointed.

Section 2. Functions of the Viral Defense Corps. (a) The VDC shall be responsible for testing the inhabitants of the United States for the Superpox-99 virus. (b) The VDC shall be responsible for categorizing citizens as either infected or virus free. (c) The VDC shall be responsible for protecting virus-free citizens from those infected with the Superpox-99 virus.

Section 3. Authority of the Viral Defense Corps. (a) The VDC shall have the authority to perform blood-sample testing on any inhabitant of the United States. (b) Beyond enforcing mandatory testing, the VDC shall have no additional authority over those who are found to be virus free. (c) The VDC shall have the authority to detain, imprison, segregate, or take any other actions deemed necessary to prevent those who test as infected from posing a danger to the population of the United States.

President Glass stared at the paper with the same horror that a frightened man might study a contract he had just signed in blood with a Crossroads Demon. And, like that man who had traded his soul for profit, she understood that her signature on the order could only lead to eternal damnation.

She felt sick to her stomach. This was the kind of action that dictators took to tighten their grip over citizens too frightened to rebel. She had no misconceptions about what she was signing. Lincoln had carefully worded the document to give him the legal authority to enforce his brutal agenda of population cleansing. In her heart, she knew that such an action was indefensible.

Despite all her reservations, she scribbled her name at the bottom of the page. President Glass accepted that she was taking the easy way out. But she also understood that, if she fought against his agenda, she would have to propose one of her own. And that was something that she was currently incapable of doing. It was better to ride on a train headed to hell than to be left behind sitting on the cold iron tracks of indecision.

CHAPTER
14

After much discussion, Boone's church congregation formed a small council to organize and plan the town's recovery. To keep it manageable, the council was limited to ten members. Anyone with previous political experience was immediately ruled out. This was to be a council of action, and only those with practical skills that could be put to immediate use were invited. The time for politics would come later, assuming that the small society even survived.

Mason, Father Paul, Ava, and retired Police Chief Max Blue were the first four selected for the council. In addition, there were six others familiar with nearly every aspect of the city. They included a general contractor, a foreman at the local water plant, an engineering professor, an influential businessman, a tow truck operator, and a banker. Immediately following the larger meeting, the ten gathered around a long table in an antechamber of the church.

"Does anyone have a suggestion about where to start?" Ava asked, looking around the table.

Despite the seriousness of the situation, Mason couldn't help but be drawn in by her exotic beauty, the long black hair, rich brown skin, and trim runner's body. She noticed him staring at her and smiled.

Caught in the act, he instinctively looked away. Regretting his retreat, he looked back to see that her eyes had never left him. He nodded slightly, and she did the same.

Collecting himself, he said, "Survival starts with food, water, and shelter. In this case, shelter isn't much of a problem. That leaves food and water."

"At the hospital, we're already seeing signs of dehydration as well as a host of stomach ailments caused by drinking contaminated water. Access to clean water would really help."

Fred Turner, a man with a large belly and a full beard, said, "I was a supervisor at the water treatment plant. If I had electricity and a few helping hands, I could get the city water back up and running within a day. The

The Survivalist   Arthur T. Bradley pressure might not be as good as what people are used to, but at least the water would be flowing."

"Based on our turnout, getting the helping hands shouldn't be a problem," said Father Paul, "but I'm not so sure about the electricity. That's an infrastructure that is generated beyond this small town."

Betty Laslow, a petite middle-aged black woman, and professor at the university, spoke up.

"We have a large solar generation system at the college, but I'm afraid there are very few people left who still know how to operate it."

"Even if we could get it operational, it would be a major undertaking to tie it into the existing distribution system," said Fred.

"Don't you have backup generators to run the water pumps in case the power goes out?" asked Mason.

"We do, but the fuel ran out more than a week ago."

"There must be at least two dozen gas stations in town," Chief Blue pointed out. "Can't we get at least one up and running?"

Steve Price, a foreman who had run several large city construction projects, spoke up.

"It shouldn't be too hard to get a generator over to one of the service stations and wire it up."

"Once you get a fuel pump running," asked Mason, "can you truck the gas over to the water plant?"

"Sure. My sons and I can do that."

"If you bring me the fuel," said Fred, "I'll get the water turned back on. But we'll need a couple of people at the plant around the clock to keep everything running."

"A small price to pay for clean water," said Father Paul. "In my mind, water may be the single biggest step we can take to ease suffering."

"It's important that we think about the long term, too," said Mason. "Even if the water plant is brought back online, the fuel will eventually run out. I'd suggest that we find some way to stockpile as much water as possible."

"That's easy," said Fred. "We have the two old water towers on the outskirts of town. Together, they hold nearly a million gallons. If we can get the pumps running, the system can refill them in a matter of days."

"If the townspeople are frugal, a million gallons could last a good many months," said Mason.

"Especially given the town's current population," said Betty. Her hand flew to her mouth. "I'm sorry, that was terribly insensitive."

Father Paul touched her hand and offered an understanding smile.

Without further discussion, everyone agreed to the plan, and actions were assigned. If all went well, water would be flowing by the following morning. A few days after that, the town's water towers would be full, providing a critical safety net.

"Next on the agenda is food," said Father Paul, rubbing his belly. "I, for one, would love a hot meal."

"There's plenty of food to go around for a while if it can be safely gathered from people's homes and grocery stores," said Betty. "So many people died so quickly . . ." She left the rest unspoken.

Father Paul didn't seem convinced of the plan. "Gathering food from homes would require a huge team of people. Plus, we'd need someplace to store and serve the food."

Betty was quick to reply.

"I was thinking that the cafeteria at the college would be an excellent place to serve food. Even if we can't find a way to get the ovens running, we have tables and other commercial food preparation equipment."

"Once again, it will come down to getting enough people to support this," said Father Paul. "They're going to be afraid, especially to go into other people's homes."

Mason turned to Ava.

"How long does the virus stay alive in dead bodies?"

"Strictly speaking, a virus isn't alive at all," she said. "A virus is a particle that infiltrates a living organism, replicates, and eventually kills or mutates the cells. But, in answer to your question, I'm not really sure. Certainly, smallpox was contagious through exposure to bodily fluids, even after death. However, it appears that Superpox-99 may be different."

"Why do you say that?"

"I've spoken with numerous people who have come into contact with bodies, either burying them, or simply moving them out of their homes. In every case, they didn't contract the virus. It appears that, when the host dies, the virus quickly becomes inactive."

"Thank God for that," sighed Father Paul. "I personally removed nearly two dozen bodies from the church yesterday."

Everyone looked around the church, and, for the first time, understood the importance of the question at hand.

"I'm confident that infection becomes unlikely a few hours after death," Ava continued. "That's one reason I believe that this virus isn't naturally occurring."

Mason leaned forward in his chair.

"Are you saying that you think this is a biological weapon? A terrorist attack on our country?"

She shrugged. "I suppose it could be, but it seems more like an accident to me. Think about it. Every country in the world appears to have been equally devastated. That's not much of a military strategy."

"People playing God with things they can't control," said Chief Blue.

"Amen," agreed Father Paul.

"If it is a bio weapon, it makes sense that it might have been engineered to spread quickly, kill nearly everyone, and then die out in a controlled manner," said Mason. "That would have enabled the users to have some certainty about when to emerge from hiding."

"So, are we safe to gather food from homes?" Betty looked skeptical.

"It sounds like the answer is yes," said Father Paul. "But, just to be on the safe side, we should warn everyone to stay clear of any bodily fluids." He turned to Betty. "If I get you a small army of helpers to collect and prepare food, can you run the cafeteria?"

"Yes, of course. I'm happy to be responsible for keeping people fed. We'll set it up like a soup kitchen. No one goes home hungry—that's my pledge," she said, holding up her hand as if taking a solemn oath.

"As for the long term," added Father Paul, "we're going to need to get seeds in the ground. It's almost spring, so at least the timing is in our favor."

Steve said, "There are tractors all around the county just sitting idle. We could set up several large communal gardens to help feed the town through this coming year. I think we should also suggest that individual families establish their own small gardens. Many of us have farming in our blood, so I'd be surprised if we couldn't make a go of it. That said, it would require that nearly everyone learn to work the land."

"What could be more important than eating?" said Mason. "People need to understand that if they don't grow it, they won't eat. It's that simple."

Again, a plan was quickly drawn up and assignments issued. By the following evening, the college's cafeteria would start serving a single evening meal to anyone who was hungry. Seeds from the local cooperatives would be gathered and rationed out to the townspeople so that everyone would have what they needed to put food on their tables through the coming year.

"Next on the table is a more . . . difficult subject," Father Paul said, a little sheepishly. "We have to do something about the dead." He looked around the table, and many looked down at their hands. "It took me nearly a full day to carry out the bodies in the church. And, may God forgive me, but they're piled out back like bags of old clothes. Despite my best intentions, proper burials just weren't possible. I will need help putting them to rest."

"The bigger question is what to do with all of the bodies?" asked Ava.

Everyone looked around the table, but no one seemed to have a solid answer.

"Perhaps we could burn them in a giant bonfire?" suggested Chief Blue.

Steve shook his head.

"The amount of fuel required would be tremendous. I know it sounds awful, but you're better off burying them in a big pit somewhere. I have a couple of bulldozers that could be put to use."

"A mass grave?" whispered Betty, horrified. "We're talking about our friends and family. They deserve better than that."

"I'm open to ideas," said Steve. "If I had to guess, I'd say we have about fifteen thousand bodies in and around the city. That's a whole lot of grave digging."

"Fifteen thousand is probably pretty close," agreed Ava. "That would put our current population at around two thousand."

"Fifteen thousand dead sounds impossible for us to handle," Chief Blue said more to himself than those at the table.

"Maybe there's another way," Mason said, rubbing his chin.

Everyone turned to him.

"What if we clear and bury only those bodies that are truly in the way? Leave the others where they lie. Within a few months, there won't be anything left but bones and hair. You could clear the remains out later without having to deal with the bodily fluids."

"But we'd have cars and homes all around us, with decaying bodies inside," stuttered Betty. "How can we expect people to live like that?"

"They're already living like that," countered Ava.

"Look, I understand it's not ideal," said Mason. "But, for a while, people are going to have bigger concerns. If we can clear the homes of bodies where there are still survivors, as well as any businesses or public venues that might be viable, it will be enough for now."

"We could use police tape or paint to mark off houses that shouldn't be entered," offered Chief Blue. "And the bodies that are removed could be buried over at Winkler cemetery. Maybe not one to a grave, but we could get them in the ground where they belong."

"Given some time, I could clear the major streets by towing the cars with bodies to keep-out zones at the edge of town. Auto grave yards, if you will," volunteered Big Al, the owner of a tow-truck service company.

"Will you need help?" asked Father Paul.

"Nah. The missus and I can do it. But we could probably only move about ten cars a day, so it will take some time." He turned to Steve Price. "We'll be needing some of that fuel, too."

"Understood."

"So, it's settled then," said Father Paul, looking around the table to see if anyone objected. When no one spoke up, he said, "Chief Blue, will you take point on marking the houses and coordinating disposal of those bodies that absolutely must be moved?"

The retired police chief nodded.

"Next on the list is security," said Father Paul. "As you heard, people are afraid not only of the virus but also of the strangers who have taken over our town. Convicts, criminals, call them what you will—they're terrorizing everyone."

"People should be afraid," said Betty. "These are awful men."

"Fortunately, Marshal Raines has volunteered to help us with this very serious problem."

Mason took his time to make eye contact with each person at the table, trying not to linger when he met Ava's eyes.

"I hope that everyone appreciates that this is going to be a difficult conversation. We're talking about setting up a rule of law that has punishments that we will have to administer."

"Marshal, we'll need to start by making it clear what those rules are. We can't just assume that people know what's allowed. Many people, myself included," confessed Chief Blue, "are taking things from abandoned stores, cars, and homes in order to survive. Are we going to allow that to continue?"

"Chief, we're all doing what we need to survive," said Mason. "We don't want to get in the way of that, but we must establish a set of basic laws to provide a measure of safety to the townspeople."

"Like the Ten Commandments," said Father Paul.

"Exactly. We'll keep it simple by outlawing violent crimes, including murder, rape, assault, and robbery."

"Is it really necessary to tell people not to murder?" murmured Betty. "What's happened to our humanity?"

"I can tell you that some people have no humanity," Ava said, shaking her head. "Violence is occurring every day in Boone. Gangs of men are raping young girls, some no older than ten. People who have been infected are being shot for target practice."

"What will we do with the lawbreakers?" asked Chief Blue. "It's not as if we can toss people in the city jail to await trial."

"The way I see it is we really only have a few sticks," said Mason. "For the most minor offenses, we'll mandate some form of community service, basically giving them a second chance. We certainly have lots of work to be done. More serious crimes will lead to banishment from town. Finally, the most violent offenses, including rape and murder, will be dealt with on the spot. No trial. No second chances."

Charlie Buttons, the owner of several ski rental stores, blurted out, "My Lord. You're proposing some kind of brutal frontier justice."

"That's exactly what I'm proposing. If you'd prefer, we can have Ava and the other doctors castrate the rapists," Mason said without the slightest hint of a smile.

"I'd be happy to," she replied, biting her lip to suppress a grin.

"And who will kill these criminals?" demanded Charlie. "You, Marshal?"

"My deputies and I will be responsible for enforcing the law."

"This doesn't sound right," said Charlie. "We're better than this."

"Charlie, do you have any family still alive?"

He seemed surprised by the question.

"Why, yes. My eighty-year-old mother and both my sons survived the virus."

Mason leaned forward, resting his forearms on the table.

"I want you to imagine that a gang of men grabbed your eighty-year-old mother. Beat her. Raped her. And then cut her throat. Imagine that for me."

"You're disgusting," Charlie sneered, staring hard at Mason.

"What would you have me do to such men?"

"That's insane. That would never happen."

"Or maybe one of your sons is brutalized. Evil can do unspeakable things when left unchecked. On my way into Boone this morning, I found a young man whose face had been bashed in with a hammer. His wife or girlfriend was taken, almost certainly raped and murdered. Again, I ask, what justice is fair?"

Charlie looked down at his hands resting on the table.

"I don't know, Marshal. I'm a man of peace. I . . . I don't know about these things."

Mason's voice softened. "We're living in a new world, one that, for the time being, will require this frontier justice that you've described. It's not something anyone should be comfortable with, but it is the only way forward."

Hoping to diffuse the tension, Father Paul said, "Marshal Raines, can we trust that you will be judicious in your use of force?"

Mason nodded, his jaw set hard.

"You have my word that I will be only slightly more vicious than my enemy."

Tanner drove east on Highway 20, the red Honda Odyssey minivan slowly navigating the congested road, like a mouse working its way through an experimenter's cruel maze. For the past ten miles, the number of abandoned cars had been steadily increasing, and, while the interstate was still passable, it never allowed him to exceed ten miles an hour.

The two rows of rear seats had been folded down, and Samantha lay resting in the back with a couple of blankets draped over her.

"It's not very comfortable back here."

"And yet you slept," he said, catching her eye in the rearview mirror.

"Evidently, being in a helicopter crash makes you tired. How far have we gone?"

"About eighty miles. We'll be coming up on the outskirts of Atlanta soon."

Samantha climbed up into the front passenger seat, pulling one of the blankets with her.

"Are we going to drive straight through?"

"No. We'll get on the 285 loop and go around the city."

"Why not go through the middle? Wouldn't it be quicker?"

"Atlanta had roughly five million people living there when this thing hit. You can imagine how bad it must be."

"Oh, right. Okay, let's go around."

"At this rate, though, it will take several hours."

She looked out the window.

"We won't make it before dark."

"Another reason to stay out of the city."

After a moment, she said, "I'm sorry, but I really need a bathroom break."

"Okay."

They drove in silence for a few minutes. When Tanner spotted an exit that was still passable, he pulled off the interstate. A McDonald's restaurant and two gas stations came into view. He pulled into the parking lot of the larger of the two gas stations.

"Let's hit the restroom and maybe grab a few snacks," he said.

They got out of the van and approached the store. Surprisingly, it was still in remarkably good shape. There were a couple of deserted cars out front, but the glass door to the store was unbroken, as were its large windows.

Tanner gave the door a push. It didn't budge.

"Try somewhere else?" she asked.

"Give me a sec." He went back to the van and returned with a small crowbar.

"You don't mind breaking into places, do you?"

He cut his eyes toward her.

"If you'd rather pee in the bushes, that's okay with me."

"I was just making an observation."

"Uh-huh." Tanner slipped the blade of the pry bar between the door and the jam, and leaned into it. The doorframe bent and the bolt pulled free of the striker plate. He gave the door a gentle push, and it swung inward. "We're in."

"Two thieves in the night," she muttered under her breath.

Even with the limited light remaining, it was clear that the store had been cleaned out. Shelves were mostly empty, and the glass coolers had only a few bottles lying in the bottom.

"Not much here," he said. "Let's hit the restroom before it gets too dark."

He led Samantha through the store until they found the door of the women's bathroom. "Let me check it."

"Okay, but please hurry. I've really got to go."

He swung open the door, but immediately closed it when the stink of human decomposition poured out.

"Let's check the other one."

She followed him to the men's bathroom door. He opened it, and this time, there were no unusually foul odors. He stepped inside and looked around, handing the door to Samantha to hold open. The bathroom was a simple single-room unit. No one, living or dead, was inside.

"I doubt that the water will run," he said, stepping back out.

"I'll manage."

Tanner grabbed an empty milk crate from the hall and wedged the door open.

"I'll get what I can from the store."

Less than a minute later, Samantha came out of the restroom.

"Better?" he asked.

"Yes. What did you find?"

"Let's see, I've got a few Slim Jim beef sticks, some licorice, and about half a dozen purple sports drinks. We can check the other store, too."

"Let's just keep moving."

"Fine. Wait for me while I hit the can."

She opened one of the drinks and began sipping it.

Tanner went into the bathroom and relieved himself. When he came back out, Samantha was gone.

He scanned the dark room to make sure that his eyes weren't playing tricks on him. She was nowhere in the small store. He raced out of the building, looking left and right. A man shuffled across the dark street, carrying Samantha under his arm like a prize he'd won at the county fair. Tanner sprinted after him.

He caught up to the stranger before he had even finished crossing the four-lane road.

"Put her down!" he bellowed.

The man spun around, panting from the exertion of trying to run while carrying an eighty-pound girl. He was disfigured in a way that no man should have been able to survive, let alone endure. Deep pockmarks permanently disfigured his face like craters on the surface of the moon. His eyes were swollen and oozing a black, inky fluid from their corners.

Samantha was kicking and screaming, fighting to get free.

"Put her down," Tanner repeated.

"You stole my daughter," the man said, still trying to catch his breath. "Took her from me while I slept."

Samantha finally broke free and fell to the ground. The man reached for her, but she quickly scooted away. When she was far enough away, she scrambled to her feet and ran around behind Tanner.

The man looked utterly distraught and reached out his arms to her.

"Jenny. Jenny, come here." He took a step toward them.

Tanner struck him with a short heel palm to his chest. The man stumbled back and fell on his backside. He sat there, holding his disfigured face, crying, "Jenny, Jenny, my dearest Jenny. Where are you, Jenny?"

Tanner and Samantha slowly backed away, watching him until they made it back to their van. Without saying a word, they loaded up and drove back onto Highway 20.

When Samantha's heart finally stopped pounding like a Japanese Taiko drum, she said, "What do you think was wrong with him?"

"The virus, I guess."

"He scared me."

"He was ugly enough to scare Frankenstein."

She choked out a little laugh.

"Thank you for not killing him."

"Huh?"

"He seemed to be a very sad man. I don't think he needed killing."

"Despite what you might think, I don't go around killing people."

"Sometimes you do."

He sat quietly, letting her words sink in.

"Yeah," he said, "sometimes I do."

"Do you think . . ." Her voice trailed off.

"What?"

"Well, he carried me with his hands."

"Ah, and you're wondering if you might be infected. Is that it?"

"I don't want to end up like him."

"You won't."

"How do you know?"

"His face was scarred, not blistered like others we've seen."

"So he wasn't contagious anymore?"

"I wouldn't think so."

"But you're not sure."

"Do I look like an expert on viruses?"

"No, you look like a football player."

"Thank you. That's the nicest thing you've ever said to me."

"So, you're pretty sure?"

"Yes, I'm pretty sure. And if I'm wrong, you'll turn into a cheese face."

She laughed. "If I do, you will, too."

"Maybe, but I'll look good as a cheese face. Probably marry a cheese-face lady and have a house full of cheese-face kids."

She smiled and looked out the window.

They drove for another thirty minutes, silently witnessing the growing pandemonium of the interstate. Cars were smashed into one another, flipped upside down, and sitting at every possible angle. Tanner steered the van onto the shoulder and navigated the wreckage as best as he could, but it was becoming more and more difficult. He wasn't entirely sure that the road would even be passable closer to the city.

Still looking out her window, Samantha said, "There are dead people inside a lot of these cars."

"Yes."

"And flies eating on them."

"Don't look if it upsets you."

"I didn't say it upset me."

"You didn't have to."

"I suppose you don't get upset by seeing dead bodies."

"It depends on who's dead."

Before she could reply, they slammed to a stop. She smacked the dash with her hand, which was the only thing that saved her head from hitting the windshield. Tanner had bumped one of the cars he had been trying to pass, and it spun around to wedge itself against the side of their van. He gave the van some gas, but the tires spun as the other car held them in place. He popped it in reverse, but again, the tires couldn't find the necessary traction.

He opened the door.

"Where are you going?"

"To see if I can get us free."

"But—"

"But what?"

"Nothing," she said, leaning back against her seat.

He stepped out and walked around to the other side of the van. The car had wedged its bumper under the wheel well of the van. He squatted down and examined the damage. It looked pretty bad. Even if he could get it free, the van's front passenger-side tire had been damaged. He couldn't chance driving on it. He went to the Samantha's window and motioned for her to roll it down.

"Don't tell me," she said. "We're stuck."

"We'll need to swap to another vehicle."

"But they all have dead people inside."

"Then we'll walk until we find an empty one that I can drive out of this mess."

"But it's almost dark."

"I don't really want to spend the night—," Tanner suddenly whipped around, his hands at the ready. He peered into the darkness but saw nothing more than the death and destruction he had witnessed for the past fifty miles. The only difference was that now he was standing exposed, right in the middle of it.

"What is it?" Samantha's voice was shaking.

"Nothing."

"Then why did you turn around? You heard something."

He scanned left to right and then back again. Nothing.

"Probably just a car settling."

"Or a zombie."

He looked at her.

"You're afraid of zombies?"

"Everyone's afraid of zombies."

"I'm not," he said, moving around to the back of the van.

"Yes you are," she shouted out the window.

"Nope," he said, popping open the hatch. "I eat zombies for lunch."

"No one eats zombies," she said, quickly stuffing her backpack with supplies. "They get eaten by zombies."

"Not me." He loaded his own pack and slipped it on his back.

She climbed out of the van and came to stand beside him.

"You're telling me that if a horde of zombies started climbing out of these cars, you wouldn't be afraid?"

"Nope. Not one bit." He started walking down the interstate and she followed close behind him.

She seemed beside herself. "A horde? A whole horde?"

Tanner grinned.

ఇం ఇం

They walked for more than twenty minutes without finding a car that was both easy to access and devoid of the dead. It seemed that everyone had been trying to escape Atlanta, for obvious reasons, and was inadvertently trapped in the mass exodus. Like a crowded theater in which someone shouts, "Fire," panic had claimed its fair share of victims.

The whole time they walked, Tanner had the nagging feeling that they were being followed. He didn't bother stopping to survey the cluster of overturned cars and debris. The road had become so utterly dark that it was like swimming through a barrel of oil. The only light was the soft glow of moonlight and the colorful glints as it bounced off car reflectors.

The most disturbing part, however, was not the darkness. It was the strangeness of the sounds around them. Their footsteps crunched across asphalt covered in broken glass. Cars creaked and moaned, protesting their unfortunate doom. And a steady wind whistled through the wreckage like the haunting cry of a sleepless witch.

Out of the blue, Samantha asked, "Do you think I'm annoying?"

"Yes."

"No, really."

"Yes, really."

"Humph."

They walked a little longer.

"You don't like me then?"

"I didn't say that."

"So, you do like me?"

"I didn't say that either."

"You can't have it both ways. Either you do—"

A low growl sounded from up ahead. Tanner stepped directly in front of Samantha.

"Hush, now."

The growl sounded again, this time closer. Another growl came from their left. And then another behind them. Tanner saw the unmistakable shine of eyes coming out of the dark.

Scanning the cars around him, he looked for a place to hide. The best he could find was a green Mustang with a badly smashed front end. Without saying a word, he scooped Samantha up in his arms and ran for the car. He could hear the unmistakable scratching of something coming up behind them. Tearing open the door, he tossed her in and fell in behind her. Powerful jaws grabbed the cuff of his jeans and tried to pull him out. He kicked backward, missing his target but tearing his clothing free of the creature's mouth.

The head of an enormous pit bull terrier shoved its way into the car, biting viciously at his kicking leg. Tanner sat up, grabbed the door handle, and tried to slam it shut. It closed on the dog's neck, and the animal yelped in pain. He opened it a few inches to see if the dog would retreat. It didn't. He slammed the door again, this time so hard that it broke the animal's neck. It dropped instantly onto the seat, as if a switch had been flipped off in its brain.

Tanner kicked the dog's body out of the car and quickly shut the mangled door.

"Are you okay?" asked Samantha, her voice shaking with fear.

Tanner felt his leg. His pants were wet with saliva as well as torn in a couple of places, but he was uninjured.

"I'm good."

Another dog suddenly sprang out of the dark, its front legs propping against Samantha's window. It barked ferociously, large strands of slobber spraying onto the glass.

She recoiled, pressing back hard against Tanner.

"They can't get in," he said, wrapping his arms around her.

A large German shepherd jumped onto the hood of the car, barking and scratching at the windshield.

Samantha buried her face in Tanner's chest.

"But what if they do?"

He pulled her close.

"Then I'll kill them."

Mason decided to stay in Boone for the night. Not only would it save him the long, slow drive back to the cabin, but it would also allow him to check out the town after dark. At Father Paul's insistence, he agreed to sleep in one of the Church's small dorm rooms once reserved for nuns.

A few hours past nightfall, Mason and Bowie went for a walk around town. Mason carried a small flashlight but kept it off except when navigating particularly congested areas. Bowie stayed close by his side, and Mason wasn't sure if that was because he was being protective, or simply afraid of exploring a town that was creepier than the Byberry Mental Asylum.

They walked down King Street for the better part of a mile before coming upon a group of men carefully making their way along the sidewalk. Several of them carried pillowcases with goods stuffed inside; others were pushing shopping carts. They stayed close to one another and continually surveyed the street. When they saw Mason and Bowie, they came to a complete stop.

Mason clicked on his flashlight and pointed it at the men's feet so as not to blind them.

"Good evening," he said.

After a brief pause, one of the men said, "Evening, Marshal. We're glad to have you out here."

The men hustled past, obviously unsure that his presence in any way guaranteed their safety. Bowie sniffed them as they passed but gave only a soft growl.

Mason continued on. The night was cool and extremely quiet. The nearly impenetrable darkness was only broken by flickers of flashlights, candles, and lanterns as people made preparations for the night.

After another few blocks, Bowie cut in front of Mason and stopped, his nose lifted high in the air.

"What is it, boy?"

Bowie looked left and right, taking short sniffs of the cold night air.

Suddenly, there was movement from across the street. Mason instinctively drew his pistol with one hand and flicked on his flashlight with the other. Bringing them together, he scanned left and right, the white light forcing its way through the darkness like a train through fog.

A hunched figure stumbled out of a car and fell to the ground. Bowie leaped forward and let out a tremendous bark. Mason moved a few steps closer, keeping both his light and Supergrade pointed at the man. The figure scrambled to his feet, standing bent over and shielding his eyes from the blinding light.

"No, no, no," he mumbled.

As Mason got closer, he saw that the stranger was cloaked in a white blanket, resembling something that might be worn by ancient Arthurian druids. The man held his hands up in an attempt to shield himself from view, but, in doing so, revealed skin covered in a thick layer of scabs.

"Don't kill me, Marshal," he begged. His voice was garbled and hard to understand as if he was chewing a mouthful of worms.

"Why would I kill you?"

"I'm an abomination," he whined.

"You survived the pox?"

"Yes," he whispered.

"Let me see you."

"Only if you promise not to kill me."

"I'm no murderer."

"Not even a mercy killing. Promise me."

It pained Mason to hear the terrible anguish in the man's voice.

"I promise."

The man stood and pulled the blanket down to his shoulders. What Mason saw was nearly indescribable. Every square inch of the man's flesh was covered with layers of festering sores, blisters upon blisters that had ruptured, only to reform again. His eyes were opaque and milky, his hands twisted from advanced rheumatoid arthritis.

Mason hardly heard himself utter the words, "My God."

The man quickly pulled the blanket back over his head.

"You promised."

Mason struggled to collect himself. "I would no sooner kill you than I would kill my dog." He patted Bowie to emphasize the point and to let the animal know that they were not in immediate danger.

The man scoffed with doubt.

"What's your name?" asked Mason.

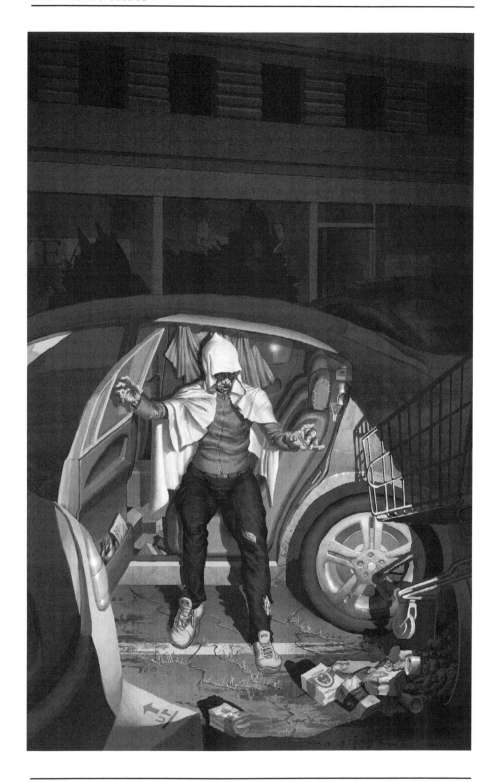

"Erik. And I know who you are. You're the lawman from the church. I watched you from the shadows."

"Who's caring for you, Erik?"

He laughed, but it sounded sick and cruel, like a torturer who had discovered a new instrument of pain.

"They would sooner put a torch to me than offer a single drop of water or morsel of food."

While Mason had heard nothing of such ostracizing, he could perhaps understand it. Fear could drive people to do indefensible things.

"Are you alone?"

The man looked left and right.

"No," he muttered. "There are others." Without another word, he turned and shuffled away into the darkness.

Mason wanted to follow him, to offer Erik something that would ease his suffering. But as he watched the man disappear into the shadows, he found himself without word or action.

ॐ ॐ

It took nearly an hour of walking in the cool nighttime air for Mason to clear the image of Erik from his mind. No one should have to live with such disfigurement. He thought back to the three people lying dead in the truck near his cabin. It made sense now why they might have felt compelled to commit suicide. Death was sometimes preferable to a life of misery.

A light coming from a major side street drew his attention. He turned and motioned for Bowie to follow. When he got close enough, he could make out the Watauga County Hospital. The large overhead sign was dark, but a glow of light came from inside the entrance to the emergency room.

Mason approached the sliding glass doors and saw that they were propped open with two large garbage cans.

"Wait here," he told Bowie.

The dog cocked its head sideways.

"Don't play dumb," Mason said, walking into the emergency room.

Bowie flopped down behind one of the garbage cans with a loud sigh.

The scene in the emergency room could have been that of hospital in a Third World country. Lighting was provided purely by candles in glass jars placed strategically around the large room. A dozen or more people were sitting or standing, obviously awaiting their turn for medical care. An old woman wearing cowboy boots and scrubs sat at a small folding table immediately inside the door. She had on a disposable facemask and vinyl gloves and was busy writing something in a logbook. She was humming a song that Mason would have sworn was "Sweet Home Alabama."

He stopped and stood patiently in front of the table.

When she finally looked up and saw him, she scrambled to her feet, pulling off her mask and gloves.

"Leave it to a lawman to sneak up on an old woman."

"I'm sorry."

"Don't be. Sneaking up means that you're up to no good, and I like men who are up to no good." She winked.

Mason wasn't sure of what to say, so he just smiled.

"What brings you to our little slice of heaven?"

"I was taking Bowie out for a walk and saw the lights."

"Your dog is here, too?"

Mason pointed toward the door.

"You know, when I was a little girl, we had a Great Dane that was probably about his size. Sweetest animal you could ever find. I used to dress it in my sister's clothes." She closed her eyes and smiled. "Better times, you know?"

He nodded. "I do."

"It's wonderful what you're doing for us, Marshal. You and Father Paul have brought hope back to Boone. I swear one day they'll erect a statue of you two. Probably right down on King Street, next to that old liquor store that used to get held up every summer."

"The good Father might deserve a statue in a better part of town," he said, chuckling.

"Father Paul a godsend all right." She held out her hand. "I'm Fran by the way."

He shook it lightly. She felt frail even beyond her years, as if her bones were constructed of paper mache.

"It's nice to meet you, Fran." He looked around the room. "I'm surprised to see that the hospital is even open."

"Not to brag, but I was the one who convinced the other nurses and doctors to come back and give this a try. Of course, it's just the ER for now."

"You're a regular Florence Nightingale."

"Why thank you, Marshal. Like you and your badge, it's what I do."

"I get it. End of the world or not, we all have to do something."

"Exactly," she said. "Ava said you were a man on a mission. I can see that fire shining in your eyes."

"A lot of people seem to think I'm here to stir up trouble."

"What do they know? I say, bring it on."

Mason grinned. Fran's enthusiasm was as contagious as the lyrics to an old Billy Ray Cyrus song.

"You and the doctor were talking about me?" He envisioned Ava's beautiful face.

Fran seemed to see right through him.

"Oh my goodness, you've caught the bug."

"What do you mean?"

"It's okay," she said, giving him a shrewd look. "Poor Ava's got it, too. Bit that girl right on the tush." She laughed, and then her eyes grew wide. "My goodness, I see it now. You're here to call on her!"

He shook his head a bit too vigorously.

"No, really we just happened this way. We saw the lights—"

"Save it," she said. "I've been around long enough to know the look in a man's eye when he's wantin' a little honey. Seen it a few times myself, if you know what I mean." She winked at him again, making it that much more uncomfortable.

Mason had no idea what to say to a firecracker like Fran, so he just shrugged and said, "You caught me."

She reached up and placed her hands against his cheeks, like a mother might when inspecting a child she was sending off to school.

"You are a hunk of red meat, all right."

Mason's eyes widened. "Thank you, I think."

"You ever made love to an older woman?" Fran made her fingers into claws and scratched playfully at the air.

His head was spinning.

She started laughing and didn't stop until she was clutching her sides in pain.

"I'm just funnin' you, Marshal."

He let out a nervous chuckle.

"I know that."

"I'm sort of known for my wacky sense of humor. No harm done, I hope?"

He leaned in and kissed her on the cheek.

"No harm done."

She turned a bright shade of pink and, for once, appeared speechless.

"I'm curious," he said, hoping to redirect their conversation, "are you able to treat people who have the virus?"

She touched her cheek on the spot where he'd pressed his lips.

"Not really. We don't have anti-virals, so there's not much we can do for them. We give out pain medicine to ease their suffering. That's about it."

"Aren't you worried about catching the virus?"

"It's why we screen people at the door. But, the truth is that the virus has already passed. We haven't seen a contagious case in almost a week." She gestured to several people around the room. "Mostly, we're treating dehydration, some heart conditions, and, of course cuts, broken bones, and gunshot wounds. Without power, we can't take x-rays or MRIs, or even consistently monitor patients' vital signs."

"Still, you're helping."

She smiled. "Yes, we're helping."

Ava emerged from one of the treatment rooms and spied Mason across the room. She waved and walked toward him. She was wearing the same green scrubs as earlier in the day, and, despite being sprinkled in blood and other bodily fluids, she looked amazing.

"Marshal Raines," she said with a big smile. "What a nice surprise."

"I thought I'd walk the town a bit to see what it was like after dark."

She came close and he could smell a faint trace of perfume.

"I can tell you that all sorts of things happen around here at night," she said. "None of them good."

"Something good happened tonight," Fran said, blatantly nodding her head in Mason's direction.

Ava turned to him and rolled her eyes.

"Please don't believe a thing this crazy old coot tells you." Even as she said the words, Ava leaned over and hugged Fran.

"I think she's planning our wedding," he said.

Ava's eyes opened wide.

"Fran, what did you—"

Fran immediately sat down and started scribbling in her log.

"Get along you two. I've got work to do. In case you've forgotten, this is a hospital."

Ava surprised Mason by reaching out and grabbing his arm.

"Come on," she said with a sigh. "Let me show you around before she names our first child."

As they turned to leave, Mason heard Fran murmur, "Daniella would be nice."

Ava led him through the waiting area and into a long hallway with treatment rooms on both sides. Curtains were drawn across most of the rooms, but a few appeared to be occupied. Candles, identical to those in the waiting room, lit each of the small treatment areas. An elderly doctor with thick gray hair was leading a patient out while giving him a small bottle of pills.

Ava pulled Mason over to the doctor.

"Marshal Raines, this is the best doctor in town and my dearest friend, Chuck Darby."

"It's good to meet you, Marshal," he said. "I couldn't make it to the church earlier, but Ava speaks highly of you. We all appreciate your efforts."

Mason extended his hand, but the doctor just smiled in return.

"Forgive me," he said, "but we're trying our best to prevent the spread of germs and viruses. Without water, I find myself using hand sanitizer at least twenty times a day."

"I understand," Mason said, making a mental note to do a better job of minimizing his own exposure.

The doctor was about to say something else when a loud commotion came from the waiting room.

"Oh, no," Ava said, turning and hurrying back into the main room.

Mason and Dr. Darby quickly followed.

By the time Mason entered the waiting room, Ava was already standing face to face with a man who could have moonlighted as a World Wrestling Federation competitor. The barrel-chested goon had arms as big as Popeye's archenemy, Bluto, and a tangle of curly, black chest hair poking up through the neck of his shirt to match. His forearms were awash in dark green tattoos, and his face sported a bushy black mustache.

Fran was lying on the floor behind her small entryway table, struggling to get up.

"Get out!" Ava commanded, pointing to the door.

Bluto reached forward to grab her, but stopped short when he saw Mason.

In the two seconds that it took Mason to take everything in, three other men strode through the front door. Two had handguns in their waistbands, and the third carried a large stainless steel revolver hanging at his side like a fistful of bad news.

For a moment, no one moved. Everyone just stared, looking from one face to the next. Sensing things were about to go from bad to worse, Ava began backing away from Bluto. The patients in the room instinctively moved closer to the walls in an attempt to blend in with their surroundings.

Mason walked slowly to the center of the room, struggling to keep his heartbeat in check. Calm hearts lead to calm hands, he reminded himself.

Ava stepped back to stand beside him. Bowie peered in from outside the door. His ears were pinned back, and his tail was tucked. He was a sneeze away from ruining someone's day.

"That brute attacked my nurse," she said, as if needing to explain what had transpired.

Mason noticed Fran holding one arm close to her body. Her carefree smile had been replaced with anguish and worry. Bluto stood confidently in the center of the room, obviously enjoying the attention. His three henchmen watched Mason, not advancing any closer but not retreating either. None of them seemed to notice the giant dog standing just a few feet behind them.

Mason turned to Bluto and parted his jacket to expose his pistol and badge. He placed his hand on the butt of his Supergrade.

"The doctor made it clear that you men are not welcome here."

"We go where we want. We take what we want," Bluto said in a deep voice befitting of his girth. "If she's not nice, we may take more than just drugs." He looked over his shoulder to make sure that his men were still there. They were.

The man holding the revolver smiled at Mason, showing off a single gold tooth.

Without ever taking his eyes off the men, Mason said, "Ava, I want you and Dr. Darby to remain very still."

"Why?" she whispered.

"Because," he said in the same even tone, "it looks as if I'm going to have to kill these men, and I don't want you to get caught in the crossfire."

"You really think you're fast enough to draw on me?" the man with the revolver said, cocking the hammer back but not yet raising his pistol.

"Are you kidding me? You'll never get that hand cannon up in time."

The man's smile faded.

"I'll make this simple, Marshal," said Bluto. "Throw down your pistol, or we'll kill everyone in this room." When Mason didn't move, he said, "I mean it. We'll butcher them like pigs in a slaughterhouse."

Several people in the emergency room started to cry and lower themselves to the floor.

"How much do you weigh?" asked Mason.

"What?"

"Two hundred and eighty pounds, give or take?"

The man puffed his chest out.

"I was two-eighty when I was twelve years old."

"And you're what? Six-foot-five?"

"Are you planning on making me a suit?" Bluto laughed, looking over his shoulder to his buddies for their approval.

"No," Mason said, shaking his head. "I was just wondering how many men it was going to take to drag your giant carcass out of here."

Before anyone could take another breath, he drew his Supergrade and fired a single shot through the bridge of Bluto's nose. The man's lights went out instantly, but his body teetered for a moment as it tried to sort out the sudden lack of electrical impulses.

Mason shifted his aim and put two bullets in the chest of the man holding the revolver.

Both of the other men went for their guns. The faster of the two fumbled the draw, and the pistol fell heavily to the floor. He reached down to pick it up, but before he got it in hand, Bowie was on him. The dog knocked the man to the floor and began ripping into him with its mighty fangs.

The fourth man got his pistol in hand, but, when he brought it up to fire, he became disoriented. Mason had dropped to one knee, and by the time the man processed the change in his target, a bullet punched through his mouth and took off the top of his head.

Everything fell silent except for the terrible screams of a man being mauled by a one-hundred-and-forty-pound animal with a head the size of a cannonball.

↾ ↽

Mason and Ava sat outside on a stone bench in the hospital's garden. Soft rays of candlelight from the emergency room spilled out to provide just enough illumination for them to see one another. The night was filled with the sounds of insects and Bowie's incessant licking as he worked to clean his paws.

"That was horrible," she said, her voice shaking almost as much as her hands.

"I'm sorry."

"As a doctor, I've seen things that would repulse any normal person. But I've never been so close to that kind of violence."

"I'm sorry," he repeated, not sure of what else to say.

"The gunfire, the screaming . . . and your dog." She shook her head, trying to clear the images of the past few minutes.

Bowie looked up as if he understood that he was the topic of conversation. When Ava didn't reach down to pet him, he went back to chewing on his paws.

"I was terribly afraid. I suppose that makes me a coward."

"I was afraid, too. Does that make me a coward?"

She shook her head. "I can't imagine anyone being more confident."

Mason said nothing as he looked out into the night. He was thankful that she couldn't see the relentless procession of "what ifs" that were marching across the parade ground of his mind.

"How did you get so good with a gun?"

"I train," he said, simply.

"I wouldn't have thought it possible for one person to defeat four."

"You're forgetting about Bowie," he said, leaning down and patting the dog. Bowie started to rise for more attention, but Mason motioned for him to lie back down.

"Even without your dog, those men never stood a chance."

Mason shrugged. "Most people don't realize that reaction is slower than action."

She looked confused.

"It just means that the person who moves first generally wins."

"So, you move first."

"I try to."

She reached over and laid her hand on his.

"I admire your humility. Most men would be stomping around boasting about their victory." She sat quietly for a moment, never removing her hand from his.

"Is Fran going to be okay? Nothing broken I hope."

"She'll be fine. I think it bruised her spirit as much as her arm. She certainly fared better than her attacker."

"When a man the size of a boxcar starts bullying an old woman, he deserves everything he gets."

"Have you ever killed anyone before?"

"Yes."

"Many times?"

He thought of the bodies decomposing at the bottom of the ravine near his cabin.

"Yes," he repeated.

"Do you mind if I ask how it makes you feel when you take a life? I've heard soldiers say it gives them a feeling of power, even elation, at having overcome their enemy."

Mason shook his head, slowly.

"I take no pleasure in killing." He paused, collecting his words. "But I don't feel much remorse either. To be in front of my gun means a person has made choices that can't be undone, or even forgiven. It becomes a moment of reckoning, a moment of justice."

She squeezed his hand, apparently satisfied with his answer.

"You're a good man, Mason Raines, a strong man."

He looked over and saw that she was crying.

"Ava, what's wrong?"

She smiled and wiped the tears away.

"I'm sorry. I'm behaving like a little girl."

"What do you mean?"

"Look at me, holding your hand, searching for some sign of strength and security in a world filled only with death and suffering." She pulled her hand away and sat up straight. "I'm sorry. You don't need this baggage."

He reached over and put his arm around her.

"There's nothing to be sorry about. We're all trying to find hope. Despite the death, there is also life, purpose, and maybe even love."

She looked up at him, the tears still trickling down her cheeks.

"You really think so?"

"I do."

"I hope you're right."

"I am."

Ava leaned over and laid her head against his chest.

Mason pulled her close, smelling the soft hint of her perfume as it mixed with the freshly burnt gunpowder still swirling through the air.

The morning following the shooting at the hospital, Mason called his four volunteer deputies together to discuss the security of the town. They met at the Boone police department, one of the few remaining buildings that hadn't been ransacked. The front window and glass door were cracked, but they were covered with bars that helped keep them structurally intact. Fortunately, retired Police Chief Blue still had keys to the station and was able to let everyone in without any difficulty.

The inside of the small police station looked pristine, as if the departing officers had simply locked it up for the night. Portable radios sat in chargers, and papers were stacked in neat piles on the three desks. The holding cells were empty, except for long metal benches and stainless steel toilets. The town's seven police officers had all died from the virus, but they were to be saluted for closing the facility in an orderly fashion, and with a sense that, one day, it might be needed again.

Mason and his deputies sat in a small interrogation room that had also served as a break room for the town's officers. A large coffeemaker was sitting on a side table, Styrofoam cups neatly stacked beside it. Coon, the scruffy hillbilly who seemed most out of place, was slowly breaking one of the cups into small pieces and then lining them up on the table into a makeshift jigsaw puzzle.

Chief Blue said, "Marshal Raines, I heard what happened last night. It's good to see you're still standing."

"Apparently, this is the second time they've hit the hospital for drugs. We obviously need to stop that sort of crime."

"We'll have to set up patrols," said Deputy Sheriff Vince Tripp. "There are only five of us, and we'll all need down time, so coverage is going to be spotty. Best we can do is probably half on and half off at any given time."

"Agreed," said Don Potts, the Army MP. "If push comes to shove, we can always call for all hands on deck."

"I want everyone to keep in mind that our goal at this point is to prevent violent crime," Mason pointed out. "We need to start by rooting out the worst offenders. If we can do that, the townspeople will largely step up and take care of the petty criminals."

"A sense of security will go a long way to helping everyone get back on their feet. No pun intended," Don said, patting his prosthetic leg.

Mason grinned. Don seemed to be a man who could not only take care of himself but also take a joke. Such men were rare.

"Chief Blue, you know your way around this station. Can you get it up and going? We may have to bring in a few prisoners, even if just to put a scare into them."

"Sure. There are two holding cells. We could probably get three people in each if needed."

"That should be plenty. I don't expect hardcore criminals to surrender to our makeshift police force. They'll call us out instead."

"The convicts are holed up over at the Walmart," said Vince. "Evidently, they broke into the store and are now using it as a de facto headquarters."

"That's actually not a bad move," said Don. "Plenty of supplies. Food, drinks, clothing— even some over-the-counter meds."

"The question is what do we do about them?" asked Chief Blue. "Just occupying the store isn't a violent offense in itself."

"It is if they use it as a base from which to attack innocent people," countered Vince.

Mason thought for a moment.

"I think we can all agree that Boone is better off without these criminals. Let's tell them it's time to leave town."

"They're likely to just shoot us on the spot," said Vince.

"Could be."

"We should wear uniforms," said Don. "It will give us a bit more credibility."

"I have my deputy sheriff's uniform," said Vince.

"And I still have my old police uniforms, assuming I can stuff this belly into them," Chief Blue said with a chuckle.

Don rubbed his chin, thinking. "I don't have a civilian police uniform, but I suppose I could put on my old Army BDUs."

"If you guys want to wear uniforms, that's fine," said Mason. "At a minimum, everyone should carry a badge. Chief, do they keep spare badges here in the station?"

"Let me check." He hopped up and left the room. In less than a minute, he returned holding three badges and an armful of portable radios. He set everything on the table.

"I found the badges in various desk drawers. I still have mine at home, so I won't need one."

"And I'll wear my Marshal's badge," Mason said, as he passed the three badges out to his deputies. "I don't plan on being a permanent member of Boone's police force anyway."

"You're not here to stay?"

"I have other obligations. I'll help to put the town back together, but then I'll have to move on."

The chief nodded.

"Those radios could come in handy," Mason added. "Can they be made to work point-to-point with disposable batteries, or are they part of some bigger trunked system that requires a base station?"

"These particular radios haven't been used since before I left office. Unlike the more complicated systems in the cruisers, these can be made to talk unit to unit by simply selecting one of the GMRS channels. If we can drum up a few batteries, I'm confident that we can get them to work."

"I've got a huge stockpile of batteries that I grabbed from one of the hardware stores," said Don. "I'll take on the job of getting the radios up and running."

"Excellent."

"What about police cars?" asked the chief. "Three of them are parked right out front. It might be a good idea if we used them to patrol the town."

"Agreed. Keys?"

"Hanging on a peg board at the check-in desk."

"I've still got my sheriff's cruiser," volunteered Vince. "That gives us four vehicles."

"Which leaves us one short." Don looked at Mason. "Are you going to stick with your truck? I'm assuming you have a light and siren on board."

"My truck will be fine."

Mason paused to size up the men who would likely be holding his life in their hands. Each of them stared back at him with a sense of purpose. All except for Coon, who was busy polishing his badge by first breathing on it, and then wiping it with his dirty shirt.

"You haven't said much, Coon."

He looked up. "Sorry Marshal. Not much to say, I guess."

Mason smiled and nodded. He had no idea how much he could trust Coon. What would he do if they came under fire? Could he operate with any sense of authority? Or would he be a renegade hillbilly who proved impossible to control or trust? While Mason appreciated every available hand, Coon instilled a nervous energy that wasn't entirely welcome.

る～ の

"The water's on!" Father Paul shouted, clapping his wet hands together as he rushed into the cathedral.

Mason sat at a small table, cleaning his Supergrade, and Bowie was lying at his feet trying to nap the day away. At Father Paul's sudden exclamation, both looked up.

"Throughout the whole city?"

"Should be," he said, rubbing his wet hands against his face. "I'm going to take a long shower. It'll be cold for sure, but still a shower. This is truly God's work!"

"The work of God or a few hard-working townspeople, who's to quibble," Mason said under his breath.

Not hearing him, Father Paul turned and dashed back toward his room, already starting to pull the vestments over his head.

"Praise God!" he exclaimed, one final time as he disappeared around a corner.

Just as Mason finished reassembling his pistol, Chief Blue entered the church.

"You ready, Marshal?"

He worked the action a few times, reloaded the weapon with a full magazine of hollow-point rounds, and holstered it.

"Ready." He looked down at Bowie. "You should probably stay here."

Bowie rose to his front paws, his ears up straight. Even sitting on haunches, his head was well above Mason's waist.

"I mean it," he said. "If you come along, you're only going to get yourself shot."

The dog leaned over and pressed its head hard against Mason's stomach. He reached down and scrubbed the dog's neck.

"Fine, but don't say I didn't warn you."

Chief Blue, Mason, and Bowie left the church and found the other three deputies leaning against their newly acquired police cruisers parked outside.

"Does everyone have their long guns?" asked Mason.

All three men nodded.

"I've got my deer rifle," Coon added. "I trust it over any of those fancy assault rifles or shotguns we found in the police station."

"Fair enough. I can appreciate the importance of knowing your weapons."

Coon smiled, showing off his crooked front teeth.

Looking from one man to the next, Mason said, "For this to work today, we have to keep them off guard. If it ends up in a shootout, we're going to lose, plain and simple. So, unless it all falls apart, keep your eyes open but your finger off the trigger."

Everyone nodded, except for Coon, who saluted.

"Chief Blue and I will give you ten minutes to take your positions. Try not to get spotted."

With a few final parting words, Don, Coon, and Vince left in a caravan of police cars heading east.

Mason retrieved his M4 and two spare thirty-round magazines from his pickup truck. He set the rifle in the rack in Chief Blue's cruiser and both spare magazines on the seat between them.

"You ready?"

Chief Blue was sweating even though the temperature was barely in the sixties.

"I haven't shot a man in nearly twenty years."

"It shouldn't come to that."

"But it could."

"Yes, it could."

"I hope I don't let you down, Marshal."

Mason turned his gaze out the window.

"Don't worry, Chief. We'll get it done."

ॐ ✦

The distance from the Church of the Fallen Saints to Boone's Walmart was only about two miles. With the gridlock of abandoned cars, however, it took nearly half an hour. Chief Blue was a careful, methodical driver, and, as he drove, he pointed out various points in the town that had been of interest over the years. There was the famous donut shop that had won a contest for serving the best coffee in the state, the clock tower that hadn't worked in more than twenty years, and the park that college students rolled with toilet paper after every sporting event, all of which were now completely irrelevant in a town that was just trying to stay alive.

Mason had Chief Blue stop the cruiser in a parking lot a block away from the Walmart. He didn't want to roll up on a gang of armed convicts with nothing more to protect him than sheet metal doors and a glass windshield. He also had the chief turn on the cruiser's lights and siren for a full minute before they exited the vehicle. This was about delivering a message, not starting a firefight—that is, if things went as planned.

Mason, Chief Blue, and Bowie approached the Walmart on foot, slow and steady, so as not to startle anyone. Sensing danger, Bowie twitched nervously with every sound or movement, like he was leading a big cat hunt in the African Serengeti.

When they were about a hundred yards out, Mason set his rifle and magazines down behind a car. This would be his retreat position that he would try to fight his way back to, if it came to that. When they were thirty yards from the store, he motioned for the chief to hang back. Chief Blue stopped and stood ready with his rifle in hand. Mason and Bowie continued on ahead.

The Walmart's two public entrances had been smashed to the point where they were nothing more than twisted metal frames. Cars pinned several bodies against the building, as if store management had resorted to using greeters as human shields as their last line of defense.

Three men stood outside the store with rifles at the ready. As soon as they saw Mason approaching, one man turned and yelled something into the store. Within seconds, two other men stepped out through the broken doors. The first man was little more than skin and bones and was wearing a bright orange hunting vest that still had a price tag hanging from its collar. The other man looked like a supersoldier who had been cryogenically preserved since the last World War. His physique was strong and lean, and he wore military fatigues, dog tags, and an old metal helmet. A large revolver was holstered at his side.

Mason stepped forward like he might when meeting an enemy general for the purpose of negotiating their surrender.

"I'm assuming you're the one they call Rommel?"

"Your reputation precedes you, boss," said the emaciated man in the orange vest.

Mason cut his eyes at him.

"And you are?"

"I'm Slim."

"Yes," Mason said with a small laugh, "you most certainly are."

The man snarled, and Mason turned back to face Rommel, who seemed to be studying him.

"You're the lawman who killed my men last night."

"That's right."

"That was pretty impressive. Did you have help from your chubby friend back there?" He gestured to where Chief Blue was standing.

"Just me and Bowie," he said, looking down at the dog.

"You must be pretty good with that sidearm."

"It's probably better that you don't find out."

Rommel squared his shoulders and let his hands hang free at his sides.

"You know, I fancy myself a bit of a gunslinger. I wonder—" He stopped abruptly.

Mason had drawn his Supergrade and leveled it at Rommel before the self-styled gunslinger could even blink.

Rommel instinctively stepped back, his hand going to the butt of his pistol. The men behind him raised their weapons.

"I've known a few gunslingers," Mason said, lowering and studying his weapon. "Most could put three bullets in their opponent's chest before he even saw the draw." He leisurely put the Supergrade back in its holster.

Rommel growled for the men behind him to lower their weapons.

"Why are you here, Marshal?"

"I came to deliver a message."

"And what's that?"

"The townspeople of Boone are giving you twenty-four hours to clear out."

Slim giggled and kicked his feet against the side of the car.

"They are, are they? Twenty-four whole hours? That's mighty nice of them, isn't it, Boss?"

Mason looked at his watch.

"To keep it simple, let's make it tomorrow at noon. That way we won't have any misunderstanding about the time."

Rommel smiled. "Tomorrow at high noon. I like your style, Marshal. You got that whole cowboy lawman thing going for you."

"Just know that I'm serious."

"And if we don't go?"

"Then I'll come back, and we'll have a very different kind of conversation."

"You're assuming that I'm even going to let you walk away from here." He looked back at the men behind him. "One word and you and your chubby friend both die. Your ugly dog, too."

"Go ahead."

Rommel gave him a questioning look.

"Watch him, Boss," warned Slim. "He's slippery."

"You're not afraid of dying?" asked Rommel.

"Are you?"

"You're fast, Marshal, but you're a fool to think you'd get us all."

"I only have to kill you, and that I know I can do. My deputies will shoot the rest."

It took Rommel a moment to fully understand what Mason was implying. When it finally hit home, he turned his head and snarled at his men.

"Get out of the open, you dimwits. He's got snipers."

The men scrambled for cover, not sure of exactly which way the bullets might be coming. When Rommel turned back to face Mason, he found himself staring, for a second time, into the business end of the Supergrade.

"You have twenty-four hours," Mason said, leaning forward until the muzzle of the weapon tapped against the helmet on his head.

Rommel's jaw tightened. "I'm not afraid of you."

Mason smiled and tapped the helmet again.

"Yes, you are."

Tanner and Samantha stayed inside the Mustang until early morning, neither of them willing to risk going back out into the dark, not even for a much-needed bathroom break. The dogs had left after an hour of incessant barking, but Tanner suspected they were never far away.

With the first rays of sunlight, both of them were eager to get out of the car and stretch their legs.

"Think the dogs will come back?" she asked, slipping on her backpack and adjusting the straps.

He looked around, yawning.

"I doubt it, but it wouldn't hurt to find a weapon just in case. Help me look inside these cars. Someone's bound to have a gun."

They walked down the centerline of the highway peering into cars. After only a few minutes, Tanner saw a large shotgun sitting in the backseat of an old Buick. On the front seat were the remains of a middle-aged couple. The dead man's arms were still wrapped around his wife's corpse.

"Here," he said.

Samantha came over and stood beside him. She peered into the window. The bodies were in full decomposition, the soft tissue starting to fall away from the bones. Flies and maggots lined the entire front seat of the car.

"That's disgusting."

"Come on, it's kind of touching."

"Touching? There are maggots in that lady's ear!"

Tanner laughed.

"I'm serious," she said. "I'm not standing anywhere near you if you open that door."

"Suit yourself."

She made it a point to count out ten large steps away from him.

"If you get stuck in there," she called back to him, "I'm leaving you here. Just so you know."

"Where's my faithful kemosabe?"

"Way over here," she said, pointing to the ground.

Tanner opened the Buick's rear door and stepped back. Waves of buzzing blowflies swarmed out like bats emerging from their subterranean hideaway. When the black wave finally thinned, he held his breath and leaned inside the car. A Remington 870 Police Magnum shotgun, two boxes of triple-aught buckshot, and a case of bottled water lay on the back seat. He grabbed everything and carried it to the hood of a nearby car. Then he went back and closed the car door to prevent the smell from drawing the dogs.

When it was all done, Samantha walked slowly back over to him.

"It's a good gun?"

He picked up the shotgun and looked it over.

"It'll do."

"Will it kill really big dogs?"

"With these shells, this thing will kill Superman."

She nodded. "Good."

He loaded the shotgun with four shells, shucked one into the chamber, and loaded a final fifth round.

"Now, let's go find us a car."

❧ ☙

The I-285 loop around Atlanta proved to be utterly impassable to automobiles. Tens of thousands of cars jammed the freeway like Christmas shoppers pushing their way into a Black Friday giveaway. Tanner and Samantha were forced to leapfrog their way around the city, driving a vehicle until it became gridlocked and then switching to another. In the end, they spent more time on foot than in a car.

"Why do you think people didn't just stay in their homes?" she asked, stepping over a small pool of blood as if it was nothing more than a puddle of rain.

"When people are scared, they run."

"If I had to die, I'd rather be at home in bed."

"Why?"

"At least I'd be comfortable."

He nodded.

"You wouldn't?"

"Wouldn't what?"

"Want to die at home?"

"Nah, too easy. You only get to go out once. Best make it count."

"How then?"

"I don't know. Maybe in an arena with a whip and a shield in my hands." He made a whipping motion with one hand.

"Like a gladiator?"

"At least I'd go down fighting."

"You like violence too much."

"That's not true," he said, his tone slightly defensive. "I have a tendency, not a taste, for violence. In fact, my religion teaches me to try to achieve a peaceful existence while helping others."

She snickered. "You may need to go to church more often."

He frowned at her, but it slowly melted into a smile.

"So, what religion are you?" she asked.

"I'm a Buddhist."

"You're not going to ask me for money like those guys in the airport, are you?"

"Wrong religion."

"Oh, sorry."

"Buddhism teaches people to come to terms with, and perhaps reduce, the level of suffering in this world."

She looked around. "This is a lot to come to terms with."

"It is."

"My mom says we're Protestants. I think that means we argue too much, but I'm not really sure."

The soft *pat-pat-pat* of a helicopter sounded in the distance. Both Tanner and Samantha stopped walking and searched the sky.

"You hear that?"

He nodded, spying the helicopter coming their direction.

"We should wave them down," she said.

"It's probably a military chopper. They won't land for us."

"They will."

He looked at her.

"Why would they land?"

She didn't answer.

"The same reason you were crawling out of a Blackhawk when I found you?"

Still she didn't say anything.

The helicopter came closer and closer, finally circling and landing about fifty yards away. Two men hopped out, one wearing military fatigues and the other a simple black suit and tie. The pilot remained in the helicopter with the engine running. As the two men approached, Tanner took a step forward, partially blocking Samantha from their view.

The man in the suit walked up and offered his hand.

"Agent John Sparks, Secret Service."

Tanner shook his hand but didn't offer his own name.

The soldier eyed Tanner suspiciously but said nothing. He had an M4 carbine resting against his chest on a single-point sling. His finger was off the trigger, but at the ready.

Agent Sparks leaned around and looked at Samantha.

"Is that you, Sam?"

She stepped around so that he could see her more clearly.

"Do I know you?"

"I'm John. It's my job to protect you. Just like Oscar. You remember Oscar?"

"Of course I remember Oscar." She felt her head. "Does it look like I suffered brain damage?"

He smiled a big toothy smile.

"Of course not, dear. You look great. Who's your friend here?"

"This is Tanner. They let him out of prison. But don't worry. He's a Buddhist."

"Is he now?" he said, looking at Tanner.

"He's taking me to my mother."

"I see. Has . . . has he hurt you, Samantha? Touched you, maybe?"

Tanner stepped forward and hit Agent Sparks squarely on the jaw. The man stumbled to his right, like a drunk with a few too many in him, and then toppled over.

"I don't believe I like you," said Tanner.

The soldier tightened his grip on his weapon and stepped back, looking to the agent for orders.

Agent Sparks sat on the ground, wiggling a loose tooth. He tipped his head to the side and let a large mouthful of blood drip out.

"If he moves, shoot him."

When the soldier turned back and started to raise his weapon, he found himself staring down the barrel of Tanner's Police Magnum.

"Think about it."

The soldier lowered his rifle and took his hand off the grip, letting the weapon hang freely in front of him.

"You'll pay for that," growled Agent Sparks.

"My mother used to tell me to think before I opened my mouth. Yours should have done the same."

The agent slowly got to his feet, nearly falling once in the process.

"Samantha, we need to go," he said, his teeth covered in blood.

"I can't—I won't get into another helicopter," she said, stepping back behind Tanner.

"Dear, I understand that you're afraid, but there's no other way. It would take a full day to get a convoy here."

She shook her head.

"Then I'll just stay with Tanner. He'll take me to my mom."

"Samantha, I'm sorry, dear, but that's not an option. It's my job to bring you to safety. You understand, right? You don't want me to lose my job, do you?"

"I don't care if you lose your job."

He stood up straight and smoothed his clothing.

"You give me no choice then, young lady. As an agent of the government, I'm giving you a lawful order to come with me. If you disobey that order, you're subject to prosecution. Do you understand what that means, Samantha?"

"It means you think I'm an idiot."

He sighed and turned back to Tanner.

"I don't suppose you're going to be smart and just walk away."

"Do I look smart? Don't answer that."

The agent leaned in and lowered his voice.

"With one radio call, I can have a gunship raining down a living hell on you."

Tanner moved the point of aim of his shotgun to the agent's belly button.

"And with one squeeze of the trigger, I can turn you into Hamburger Helper."

Samantha touched his arm.

"Remember, peace and tranquility."

He glanced at her and then back to the two men.

"Both of you put your weapons on the ground. You can thank Sam later."

"This isn't over," Agent Sparks said, taking a semi-automatic pistol from his belt and setting it on the ground.

The soldier didn't say anything as he unbuckled his rifle and let it drop by his feet.

"I'll give you to the count of sixty to get that helicopter off the ground."

The soldier looked to Agent Sparks who gestured for him to go ahead. Sparks started to say something, but Tanner cut him off.

"Fifty-nine, fifty-eight, fifty-seven . . ."

He turned and followed the soldier back to the helicopter. As they lifted off, Agent Sparks leaned out the open door and gave Tanner the one-finger salute.

෨෨ ෧෧

Tanner and Samantha sat with their backs against the door of a shiny yellow Corvette. The proud owner sat inside, his skin sagging so badly that he could have been mistaken for one of the horrors in Madame Tussaud's wax museum. Tanner was eating a Slim Jim, and Samantha a pack of red licorice.

"So?"

"So what?"

"So, who are you exactly that the Secret Service is out looking for you?"

"You know already."

"I know that the president has a daughter named Samantha."

"You just didn't know she was so cute, right?" she said with a grin.

"I didn't know she was such a pain."

She paused, hunting for the right words, or perhaps just the right delivery.

"So, are you're still going to take me to Virginia?"

"I suppose. But that convoy he mentioned will likely show up somewhere along the way. You won't need me then."

She stood up and looked off in the direction the helicopter had flown.

"Do you think Agent Sparks will tell my mom that I'm alive?"

"I can't imagine why not."

"Good. I'm sure she's worried." She sat back down and took a drink of water.

"How'd they know where to find you?"

She gently grabbed his hand and placed it against her forearm.

"Feel," she said.

"It feels like a grain of rice is under your skin."

"They said it's a short-range wireless tracker. That if I ever got lost, it would help them to find me."

"That's good, right?"

She shrugged.

"Are you going to give me that sad childhood story? Too m... tions in the Hamptons?"

"No, not that. My mom is great. My dad's dead, but he was okay.

"I'm sorry. About your dad, I mean."

"Do you have any family?"

"A son."

"What's he like?"

Tanner looked off in the distance, reliving better times.

"He's a good man. Better than me, that's for sure."

"Is he a criminal, too?"

Tanner laughed. "Quit calling me that."

"Sorry."

"No, he's not a criminal. He's a lawman. The kind you might have found standing beside Wyatt Earp and Doc Holiday."

"He sounds very brave. Maybe one day I can meet him."

"Maybe. If he's still alive."

"Do you think he is? Alive I mean."

He shrugged. "Could be. We have a cabin. If he made it there, he could have waited this thing out."

"I hope he's alive."

"Thank you."

She grabbed another piece of licorice and started chewing.

"Sam," he said, "I have a question for you."

"Sure."

"Why didn't you go with that agent?"

"I told you. I'm not getting back in another helicopter."

"That's it?"

She looked up at him and wrinkled her brow.

"What other reason could I have for not going?"

He shrugged, taking a big bite of the beef stick.

"I just figured you liked me."

"In your dreams."

He grinned. "Okay, then what gives?"

"It's just that . . ."

"Yeah?"

"Well . . . it's just that our helicopter didn't exactly crash. I mean, we crashed, but we didn't just crash."

"What are you saying?"

"I think someone shot us down."

"Who would shoot down a helicopter with the president's daughter inside?"

"I heard Oscar and the pilot talking. They called it friendly fire. It didn't seem too friendly to me, though."

"Friendly fire just means that it was our own military."

"Oh."

"It sounds like someone doesn't want you to get home."

"Oh," she said again. "But, you're going to take me to my mom, right?"

"Yes."

"All the way? No matter what?"

He looked over and saw that there were tears in the corners of her eyes.

"No matter what," he said.

She blinked a few times and swallowed hard.

"Okay then, what else do you have to eat? I'm still hungry."

CHAPTER
19

Mason met back up with his deputies at the police station about an hour after his confrontation with Rommel. They sat around the briefing table, drinking tap water from Styrofoam cups.

Coon raised a cup to his nose and sniffed the water.

"Seems clean enough. I guess we should be thankful."

"Yeah," said Vince, "thankful." He looked over at the empty coffeepot. "Marshal, any idea when they're going to have electricity back on? I could really use a cup of coffee."

"It could be some time. Weeks, months, or even longer."

"That's a long time to go without a cup of coffee on the job," said Chief Blue. "We may have to build a fire pit or some other way to boil water here at the office. With hot water, we could make our own percolator of sorts. Men can be clever when coffee's on the line."

Without another word, Mason unplugged the coffeemaker and filled it with water from the tap. He grabbed a packet of coffee and carried everything out to his truck. When he returned, his hands were empty.

"You letting the sun work some magic on the coffee, Marshal?" asked Don.

"Actually, I have an inverter out in my truck. It runs off a couple of spare lead-acid batteries in the back. Give it a few minutes, and we'll have hot coffee."

"Serious?" said Coon. "Marshal, don't joke about something like that."

"Only the best for those helping to keep me alive."

"I'm just glad we didn't have to shoot anyone today," said Don. "I had them in my sights though, just as you instructed. If it had gone south, I could have dropped two of them pretty quick."

"I had the other two," said Vince.

Mason turned to Coon.

"If they were covering the four gunmen outside, who were you targeting?"

"Marshal, sir, I had the fellow with the big orange target on his chest."

"I thought you were supposed to be a crack shot."

"I am," he said, confidently. "That fellow was awful skinny. I would've had to hit him right in the zipper to make sure he took a bullet."

Mason chuckled. "I see."

"You think they'll leave?" asked Chief Blue.

"No, I think they'll wait for us to come again."

"Not to question your leadership, Marshal," said Don, "but is that really the best strategy? When we show up in twenty-four hours, they'll be ready."

"Who says we're going to show up in twenty-four hours?" The others sat up and looked at Mason.

"But you said . . . Ah, I get it," Don said, grinning. "We're going to let them sweat it out. Then when they figure we didn't have the nerve, we'll move on them."

"Maybe. Or maybe we'll just pick them off one at a time. When their numbers get low enough, they'll skip out in the middle of the night."

"I like the idea of keeping them on their back foot," said Vince. As he said the words, he caught himself staring over at Don's prosthetic leg.

Don saw him too and grinned.

"Just to be safe, we should keep an eye on them," said Mason.

"We could do it in shifts," offered Chief Blue.

"I'll go first," volunteered Vince.

"And I'll relieve you tonight," the chief said. "My wife won't like it, but I don't sleep much anyway."

"I'll pick it up in the morning," said Don. "We can use the radios to stay in touch."

"If they're still around tomorrow, I'm happy to take a shift, too," said Coon.

Mason glanced at his watch and smiled.

"It's coffee time."

⤳ ⤶

"Come on, this is worth seeing," Ava said, pulling on Mason's arm with one hand and carrying a folded blanket with the other. She led him up a long grassy hill located on the outskirts of town.

The sun was still shining, although it was getting late in the day. Bowie ran huge circles around them, occasionally dropping to roll around in the tall grass like a pig enjoying fresh mud. It was as nice a spring day as Mason could remember.

When they got to the top of the hill, Ava let him go and wrapped her arms around a huge Northern Red Oak.

"This is it," she said with unmistakable pride. "Well?"

Mason wasn't sure exactly what to say. It was a perfectly fine tree, standing nearly one hundred feet tall and measuring three feet across. But there were thousands of similar trees in forests all around.

"It's . . . really great."

"You're a terrible liar," she laughed. "Come take a look."

Mason moved up beside her. On the trunk were carvings of names and initials, most of them surrounded by hearts. She ran her fingers over one that read, *Jon loves Ava.*

"My first love," she said. "Jon Singer. We were only sixteen when he carved that."

Mason smiled. Everyone had a first love, and they were never forgotten.

"Did you bring me here to make me jealous?"

"Yes." She winked. "Is it working?"

"Of course. So, what happened between you two?"

"The usual stuff. Jon moved off to play college football in Tennessee, and I went off to medical school. He married a lovely cheerleader, and they even invited me to their wedding. They have two boys." Her smile faded. "I wonder if his family is even alive. Those beautiful little boys . . . "

He put his arm around her.

She turned, rose up on tip toes, and kissed him on the lips.

Mason looked into Ava's eyes and saw a deep longing. Not just for him, but for a rock to hold onto. He pulled her tightly against him and kissed her, tasting the sweetness of her lips. They stood beside the tree, kissing for several minutes, enjoying the heat of one another's body and the intimacy of their first real touch.

Ava finally pulled away.

"Tell me you love me."

"Ava . . ."

"You don't have to mean it. Just tell me." She closed her eyes, hoping to hear the words.

Mason raised his hands and cradled her soft face. He leaned in very close and kissed her gently.

"I love you, Ava. You are the most beautiful woman I have ever known. Your spirit is filled with generosity and kindness, and it is truly my honor to hold you in my arms."

She opened her eyes, and small tears glistened.

"Thank you. That was really nice."

"Ava, I felt my heart stir when I first laid eyes on you."

"Now I know you're lying," she said, laughing. "When we first met in the church, I was a complete mess from working all morning."

"No," he said, "you were radiant and real, and every person felt the kindness in your heart. Father Paul would say that's the reason you were spared. And, in this case, I would have to agree with him."

She blushed, taking his hands in hers.

"You're . . . wonderful. If God spared me because of my kindness, he surely spared you because of your strength. My father would have said you are the point of the spear that others depend on in their most difficult hour."

"Point of the spear?"

"He used that expression from time to time to describe brave men who were willing to do difficult things when others couldn't."

He kissed her again, feeling the soft press of her breasts against his chest.

"What I want to know," he teased, "is what exactly I have to do to get my name on this tree."

"We'll think of something," she whispered. She pulled away and started unfolding the blanket on the soft grass. When it was smooth, she lay down and stared up at him. Her skirt had partially opened, and one voluptuous leg protruded from underneath. "Will you share this moment with me, Marshal Raines?"

Mason stood speechless. In all his years, he couldn't remember a woman who looked more beautiful than Ava did lying on the blanket. It was as if Aphrodite herself was summoning him, and as a mere mortal, he had no hope of resisting her call.

He slipped off his jacket and hung it over a limb of the tree.

"If I said no, there isn't a man alive who would forgive me."

❧ ❧

Ava and Mason lay on the blanket, completely naked, curled up against one another like two sleeping lions. Bowie rested at their feet, eying squirrels in the tree above them.

"I'm hungry," she said in a sleepy voice.

"You should be," he laughed.

She raised up on one elbow and punched him softly on the shoulder.

"Me? You're the one who wanted do-overs."

"What can I say? Once wasn't enough."

"And twice?"

"Barely."

They both laughed and kissed again. Mason ran his hands down her stomach and along her hips.

"I have a truck bed full of food. We could build a little fire and pretend we're pioneers."

"That sounds nice," she sighed, "but I was thinking that maybe we should go check to see how Betty is doing over at the university. Her soup kitchen is supposed to be up and running."

"That's a great idea. There's only one problem."

"What's that?"

He pulled her close, feeling the heat of her body.

"We'd have to put on clothes."

She kissed him. "Well, I do. You could always go as you are, but it would give that 'point of the spear' thing a whole new meaning."

๛ ๖

A large crowd had gathered on the front lawn of the university's cafeteria. Scores of people were coming and going, and while the scene was busy, it was also relaxed. No one was shoving or grabbing; everyone seemed quite willing to wait their turn.

Mason pulled his truck up on the grass, and he and Ava climbed out. Bowie had been relegated to ride in the bed of the truck, but he didn't seem to mind. As they walked up the steep grassy hill toward the cafeteria, several people offered friendly greetings.

They sidestepped a line of more than forty people and entered the university's cafeteria. A procession of volunteer servers worked a food line much like that found at a Salvation Army during the holidays. The meal consisted of meat and vegetable stew, bread, and some kind of pudding. The stew was heated in a large pot on a burner fueled by portable tanks of propane.

When Betty saw them, she wiped her hands on her apron and hurried over. "Marshal, Ava, it's nice to see you both. What do you think?" she asked, an unmistakable look of pride on her face.

"It's wonderful," exclaimed Ava. She touched Betty on the arm. "This will bring life back to our community."

Mason nodded his agreement. "Very impressive. I see you've managed to use propane tanks to cook."

"Yes, we figured out how to transfer the propane from large tanks to the smaller, portable ones. So, assuming we don't blow ourselves up, we can keep this going for quite some time."

"What about the bread? Do you have a propane oven, too?"

"I wish. Unfortunately, the cafeteria's ovens operate on natural gas, which was shut off weeks ago. I'm hoping that we can talk about that at the next town council meeting. If we can get the natural gas back up and running, we'd really be set. For now, we're baking the bread in a large pottery kiln over in the art department."

"Very clever."

"Speaking of food, you two look hungry. Can I get you some of my homemade stew? It's pretty good if I say so myself."

"Yes, please," said Ava. "I think the marshal here has worked up quite an appetite."

Mason grinned. "Indeed, I have."

Ava gave him a playful wink, and then turned to Betty.

"I'll come with you and help. I know you're busy."

As they left to get the food, Mason saw Father Paul enjoying his dinner at one of the tables.

"Father," he said, taking a seat across from him.

"Marshal Raines, do you see the miracle that Betty has pulled off? She's a saint, I tell you."

"It is quite something."

"How did it go with Rommel?"

"Time will tell."

Father Paul finished mopping up his last bit of stew with a hunk of bread and stuffed it in his mouth.

"Umm, good," he said. "I hope you're having some."

"Ava's getting it." At the thought of some warm food, he felt his stomach start to growl.

"You and the doctor? You're a couple now?"

Mason thought about it for a moment.

"Yes, I suppose we are."

"She's quite lovely. She must see something special in you."

"My good fortune," Mason said, thinking about the past few hours he had spent with her.

"Perhaps finding love is a reward for your good deeds."

"I haven't done anything yet, Father."

"Look around, my son. This is as much your doing as anyone's. Before you arrived, the town was struggling, not only to stay alive but to find any sort of hope or faith. Now we have food, water, and maybe even safety before too long."

Mason surveyed the room. Nearly every person was smiling and talking, enjoying not only the food but also the company of their neighbors.

"This is Betty's doing. I only helped to get things moving."

"You were the catalyst. Without the spark, there is no fire."

Before Mason could say another word, Ava approached, carrying two bowls of stew with large slices of bread poking out the top. She set a bowl in front of Mason and sat down beside him.

"Good evening, Father," she beamed.

"Ava, you look absolutely radiant."

"Thank you, I feel . . . radiant." She laughed and leaned lightly against Mason. "Who would have thought it possible, given the circumstances."

"We've all been given a second chance to see the world anew," said Father Paul. "Let's hope that we can remember the lesson even after the suffering has passed."

The three of them engaged in a long conversation about everything and nothing. It was the first time in weeks that anyone had been able to relax long enough to let the unimportant matter. When it became clear that others were waiting for seats, they stood and made their way out of the cafeteria. Before Mason left, he retrieved a second bowl of stew and carried it outside.

"You really were hungry," Ava teased, knowing full well that the food was not for him.

He whistled, and Bowie came lumbering up the hill, his thick fur waving along his back like the spikes of the mythical Chupacabra. Mason put the bowl down on the ground, and Bowie didn't wait for an invitation to start devouring Betty's homemade stew.

༄ ᰔ

By the time Mason and Ava arrived at the hospital, it was nearly nine in the evening. She explained that, when the virus hit, most of the hospital's patients had died, and those that didn't were evacuated to less crowded surroundings. Since then, the hospital had become a volunteer-run urgent care center, similar to those set up in foreign countries by visiting doctors.

Doctors and nurses now came and went as their time and needs allowed. After their day out, Ava planned to work until early the next morning. She promised to see him again the following day, after she'd had a chance to rest.

Once he was sure that Ava was safe, Mason cruised around Boone in his truck for a couple of hours. He told himself that he needed to patrol the streets, but the truth was he also wanted to clear his head. There was no denying that his day with Ava had been wonderful. Their lovemaking was exciting and intimate, and she was as emotionally interested in him as he was in her.

The difficulty came from the suddenness of it all. Plans that had once been clear were now like ink on a wet page. When things were eventually tied up in Boone, his intention had been to seek out the Marshal Service and offer his hand in establishing order. He also needed to find out what had happened to his mother and father. Each of these would require his leaving Boone, and he wasn't sure how well Ava would take the news. She was clearly vulnerable and afraid, and he didn't want to leave her feeling betrayed.

By the end of his patrol, Mason had resigned himself to stop over-thinking the situation and simply let things evolve at their own natural pace. When the time was right, he would pursue his duties, as he knew he must. Until then, he would enjoy the time he had been given with Ava. In the end, she would either understand or she wouldn't, and they would part with kisses or with tears.

With a newfound clarity, Mason decided to call it a night. He turned up King Street and headed for his makeshift quarters at the Church of the Fallen Saints.

The night was turning cold, and Mason buried himself under four blankets that were as ancient as the nuns who had slept beneath them. He was just dozing off when Bowie let out a loud bark as the dormitory door burst open. Mason shot upright, reaching for the Supergrade lying on the table beside his bed. Bowie snarled viciously as he scrambled to his feet, his claws scratching against the wooden floor.

Father Paul stumbled into the room, carrying a candle in one hand and a radio in the other.

"They're coming!" he said, unable to quite catch his breath.

Detecting the familiar scent of the priest, Bowie softened his warning but remained standing between Father Paul and Mason.

"Who's coming?"

"The convicts. All of them. They're coming here! Now!"

Mason got to his feet and quickly dressed. While he was pulling on his boots, he asked, "Who called it in?"

"Chief Blue." Father Paul shoved the radio toward him. "He saw them mobilizing. They're getting ready to stage an attack. Here at the church!"

"How soon?"

"I don't know."

Mason clicked the talk button on the radio.

"Chief, what's going on there?"

After a moment, a hushed voice said, "Marshal, thank God I reached you. Rommel and his men are pulling out of the Walmart parking lot. I count eleven fully-loaded vehicles coming your way."

"How soon?" Mason asked, picking up his assault rifle and checking the chamber.

"The dark will slow them down, but they'll be to you in half an hour."

"Did you call the other deputies?"

"Yes. We're all coming to you, but I'm not sure I'm going to make it in time."

"Don't try. Work your way in behind them, but maintain radio contact. You're our eyes on this."

"Roger."

Mason pressed the talk button again.

"Vince, Don, Coon, are you out there?"

Within seconds, Vince replied, "I'm out in front of the church. Ask the good Father to let me in."

Mason gestured to Father Paul, who immediately spun around and headed toward the front door.

The radio sounded again. The reception was poor and Don's voice broke up several times.

"I'm about ten minutes—stopping at—station—ammo."

"Got it," said Mason. "Get everything you can carry, including a few spare rifles."

"Roger—will get—see you—few."

Mason waited to see if Coon would sign in. He didn't. Coon's house was out to the east, and he was most likely still out of range.

"Chief Blue, if you can reach Coon, get me an ETA."

"Let me try."

After about a minute, Chief Blue came back on.

"Coon's ten minutes behind me. He's not going to make it in time to get inside either."

Mason needed every gun he could get. He thought for a moment.

"Tell Coon to find a spot near the church with a decent vantage point. He's going to be our sniper."

"Will do."

Mason looked over at Bowie. The dog knew something was coming. It held its head high, watching his every move.

"You're in this too, boy. Your job is to make it unpleasant for anyone trying to breach the windows or doors. Can you do that for me?"

Bowie's eyes narrowed and he gave a short bark.

❧ ❦

Vince, Mason, and Father Paul huddled inside the front door of the church. Mason tapped his rifle against the heavy door.

"This door is bulletproof against anything smaller than a rocket-propelled grenade. If we can brace it, they won't get through without a battering ram." He looked around the church. "Vince, give me a hand sliding a pew over here." Together, they pushed one of the long heavy benches against the door. "Now, let's stack another one on top to brace it."

Father Paul joined in, and the three of them lifted the heavy oak pew in place.

"That should hold." Mason turned his attention to the rest of the church. Most of the windows had already been broken out and boarded up, but three along the front of the church remained intact.

"Those windows will be the first things to go when gunfire starts. We need to take them out to give us a clear line of sight."

"You mean destroy them?" Father Paul asked, not hiding his disappointment.

"I'm afraid so. We'll leave that to you, Father. Do it as gently as you want, but we need to see what's coming."

Father Paul made the sign of the cross, kissing the tips of his fingers as he finished.

"The Lord surely understands our plight and the steps we must take. They are but glass, after all."

"What other ways can they get in?"

"Just the service entrance in the back. It's not particularly well fortified. There are upper story windows, too, but I would think they'd be difficult to access. And, of course, there's the bell tower in the steeple, but, again, impossible to get up there without ladders."

"So, we need to cover three windows and a back door," Mason said, thinking out loud. "Unfortunately, we only have three shooters. That leaves us one shy." He looked at Father Paul. "Ever fire a gun, Father?"

When Father Paul didn't answer, Vince added, "An eye for an eye, and a tooth for a tooth, right, Father?"

Father Paul shook his head.

"Christ reminded us to abandon that way of thinking and to love and forgive our enemies. I'm sorry, my friends, but I cannot take another man's life."

"Even at the expense of your own?"

"Yes, even at the expense of my own life. I'm sorry."

Mason saw no need to waste time trying to convince him to change his mind. A man's convictions were usually only strengthened in times of crisis.

"Better that we know that now," he said. "Can you at least help keep our weapons loaded?"

"That I can do."

There came a heavy knock at the door. Before they could even ask, Don's voice sounded from outside.

"It's me. I need a hand with the ammo."

Together, they transferred the extra weapons and ammunition in through the windows. Don quickly followed. All told, he had brought three assault rifles, a dozen thirty-round magazines, and several thousand rounds of ammunition. It was enough to stay engaged in a prolonged firefight if they kept the weapons loaded and were careful with their shots. In addition, he had brought a shotgun and fifty double-aught shells. The shotgun would be particularly useful if things got up close and personal.

"Okay," Mason said, looking to the group, "let's load every available magazine and set up firing points at each window." He gestured to the base of the three windows. "We also need to block off the back door as best we can. The pews are too big to fit down the hall, so we'll have to use bookcases, chairs—anything else that might keep that door from opening. We'll put the shotgun at the end of the hallway, ready to point and shoot that direction should it come to that."

Vince immediately starting loading bullets into the magazines as Don worked with Mason to move an assortment of furniture in front of the back door. Meanwhile, Father Paul knocked out the remaining windows with a framing hammer, offering up a prayer for forgiveness with nearly every stroke.

After fifteen minutes, they were as prepared as the situation would allow. Fire points had been set up at each window, with spare magazines and weapons at the ready. The back door was barricaded with several hundred pounds of furniture, but no one was ready to say it would hold.

Rather than expend their energy performing meaningless tasks, each lawman sat quietly beneath his window, back to the wall and rifle in hand. Mason sat under the one closest to the front door, anticipating that much of the action would take place there. Bowie lay down beside him, resting his head on Mason's lap. The room was quiet, save for the static of the radio and the dog's heavy breathing.

❧ ❦

Mason watched a long string of lights approaching from the east.

"They're coming," he said.

His radio sounded. "Marshal, are you there?"

"We see them, Chief. How far behind are you?"

"I got out in front of them. I'm across the street from the church on the second floor of the ski shop. I can make a run for the door if you want."

"Don't bother. We've barricaded it. Just stay where you are. We'll need eyes on what's going on out there. Where's Coon?"

"I'm down about two blocks, Marshal. Just climbing into the trunk of an abandoned car. I've got the lid wedged open just a hair, so I figure I'll take my shots from here."

"Good. But keep in mind that the flash of your hunting rifle is going to give you away pretty quick. Once they know you're close, they'll come for you."

"They'll find I'm as slippery as a cat burglar covered in mayonnaise. If they do finally corner me, I'll give a good account, I promise you that."

Mason smiled. His worries about Coon's commitment were proving to be misplaced.

"Just keep your head down."

"Yes, sir, I'll do that."

The lead vehicle in a long procession pulled past the church and rolled to a stop. Another car pulled up next to it, and two others directly behind them. The remaining vehicles stopped halfway down the block and barricaded the street. Dozens of armed men climbed from the cars and trucks like the ragtag army of a Colombian drug cartel. They carried an assortment of weapons, ranging from snub-nose revolvers to double-barrel shotguns.

Slim's bright orange hunting vest made it easy for Mason to pick him out in the crowd gathering out in front of the church. Rommel was standing directly beside him. The two of them began shouting orders for the men to take up various positions. Several men ducked around the side of the building, searching for a way into the church.

"I'd like to have a word with you, Marshal," shouted Rommel.

Mason peeked through one of the broken window panes.

"I'm listening."

"Yesterday, you came to us with a demand. Today, I'm here to make one of my own."

"What's that?"

"I'm appointing myself mayor of this crappy town, and, as such, I'm giving you one chance to surrender to my lawful authority."

"And if I don't?"

"Then I will have no choice but to punish you and all those inside."

Mason looked around the room and found only determined men willing to fight.

"Well?" Rommel asked in an impatient tone.

Mason popped up and shot him in the chest.

For a moment, nothing happened. It was as if time was a vinyl record stuck spinning on the same track. Slim and the other men stood mesmerized, looking at Rommel on the ground, then back at the church, utter bewilderment in their eyes. Then the world broke loose.

Men ducked for cover. A few fired wild, uncontrolled shots at the church. Slim and two others grabbed their leader's twitching body and dragged him behind the closest vehicle. Mason was disappointed to see Rommel stagger to his feet as they helped him to safety. The only possible explanation was that he was wearing a bulletproof vest.

That's when the heavy firing started. For about twenty seconds, hundreds of rounds of every caliber pounded the walls and door of the old church. Dozens of bullets passed through the open windows, tearing up the dais and crucifix. But the solid stone walls held, and not a single round came close to anyone inside the room. To keep Bowie from getting hit by a stray bullet, Mason had to hold him down. Bowie struggled to get to his feet, but, when he saw that it was of no use, surrendered and settled to the ground.

When silence finally came again, Mason keyed the radio.

"Chief, tell me when they begin to move on us."

"Will do. You guys okay in there?"

"We're fine. Coon, you ready?"

"Yes, sir. Just waiting for go time."

"They're charging the door!" yelled Chief Blue.

Mason made a quick motion with his hand, and all three shooters rose to their windows and began firing. The sound of the gunfire in the church was absolutely deafening as Mason, Vince, and Don laid down a heavy barrage. Coon also started firing, taking his time in order to get meaningful hits. The volley of bullets left six convicts bleeding in the street and two others crawling back behind cover, screaming in pain as they went. As magazines were emptied, each man dropped back down and quickly reloaded. Father Paul shuffled across the room in a low squat, gathering up the empty magazines and taking them to his impromptu reloading area.

Mason looked over at Vince and Don.

"Good shooting. Remember, take what you can get. We don't have to kill them, just put them on the ground. Legs, shoulders, and gut shots will do just fine. There are no medics here."

A loud explosion sounded from the back of the church. Before Mason could stop him, Bowie bolted that direction, barking wildly. Mason motioned for the others to stay put as he charged after the dog. Turning the corner from the hallway, he saw that a three-foot-wide hole had been blown in the bottom of the back door. A man was crawling through on all fours, sliding a shotgun ahead of him like it was a sack of gold he had pilfered from a tomb.

Before he cleared the furniture heaped in front of the door, Bowie scrambled under and grabbed him by the top of his scalp. The man screamed and fumbled unsuccessfully to raise his weapon. Bowie dragged him into the hallway, shaking him viciously from side to side until his neck snapped.

A second man immediately scurried in through the hole, holding a pistol at the ready. Mason brought his rifle up and fired three quick shots, killing him instantly. He nodded to Bowie, who released the first man, and turned back to see if any more dared to crawl through the hole. For the moment, none did.

Mason yelled over his shoulder.

"The back door's been breached. Bowie and I will hold them here."

"Got it!" shouted Vince. "We'll give them hell up front."

A long string of shots rang out again from the front of the church. Bullets smashed into the walls and door, tearing away at the church. Don and Vince used any lull in the barrage to return fire, the sharp *tat-tat-tat* of their assault rifles echoing through the building.

Suddenly, several powerful shotgun blasts tore grapefruit-sized holes in the back door. Mason dropped to one knee and stayed close to the wall to avoid the shrapnel. Bowie stood beside him, the dog's body tense with excitement.

"Wait 'til they come through," he said.

Bowie turned his head and licked the side of Mason's face, leaving a smear of the dead man's blood on his cheek.

The body of the man lying dead in the hole was dragged backwards by his legs. Another man scrambled forward in his place, firing several shots from an assault rifle as he advanced. Mason returned fire, striking him in the neck and head. He jerked for a few seconds and then fell silent. No one else followed in what had so far proved to be a flawed strategy.

Just when Mason thought that the convicts might abandon the back door altogether, a large man smashed against it with his shoulder, splitting it in several places. Mason brought his rifle up and took aim. When he hit the door a second time, Mason fired a single shot through one of the large holes. The bullet caught the man in the rib cage, and he screamed in agony as he fell to the ground. His attack on the door, however, had had the desired effect. It wasn't going to hold much longer.

Vince and Don weren't doing much better. There were so many rounds shattering against the window frames that neither could rise up to get a clean shot. Instead, they resorted to holding their rifles above their heads and firing blindly out into the street. Father Paul was also having difficulty keeping up with the reloading because he couldn't safely traverse between the windows. They had adopted a method of sliding empty magazines to him, and, when reloaded, he would slide them back. It proved slow and ineffective because some of the magazines missed their mark and now lay in areas too dangerous to retrieve.

Vince screamed as a bullet hit his wrist, shattering it and sending a steady stream of blood down his arm. He dropped his rifle and clutched the hand, his face twisted in agony.

"I'm hit!"

Before anyone could respond, Coon's voice sounded over the radio.

"They're pressing me pretty hard. I'm ducking into one of these buildings."

Mason grabbed the radio from his belt.

"Coon, try to get to higher elevation. We need to take out Rommel."

There was no reply.

Chief Blue said, "Marshal, what can I do?"

"Give them something to worry about. We're falling apart in here."

A section of the back wall suddenly collapsed inward as a car smashed into it, sending large chunks of brick and rock tumbling inward. Dust and mortar filled the air. By the time Mason could get a clear shot at the windshield, the car was already reversing. Not only was the door now breached, but another hit would bring down the entire wall.

He shouted to the men in the front room.

"Enemy in the wire! Upstairs quick!"

Father Paul grabbed an armful of ammunition boxes and dashed for the stairs. Vince and Don took a moment to collect their magazines before bolting after him. When Don was about halfway across the room, a bullet hit his prosthetic leg, breaking it off at the knee. He toppled to the stone floor like a marionette whose strings had been cut.

Vince turned back to help him, but the onslaught of bullets forced him to resume running toward the heavy staircase.

Don rolled to his back and held his rifle at the ready.

"Go on!" he yelled. "I'll hold them as long as I can."

Without warning, Bowie darted across the room, took a firm bite of his collar, and began dragging him toward the stairs. Bullets smashed all around them.

Mason moved to the bottom of the staircase and directed Vince and Father Paul to go up and find cover. They took off like a pack of hellhounds was hot on their heels.

A convict wearing a black ski mask started climbing through the window closest to the door. Still lying on his back, Don shot the man twice in the chest. Another man dove through the second window, landing hard on the shotgun he was holding. Mason fired three rounds as the intruder scrambled to his feet. Two bullets hit him in the hip, and a third took off the top of his head.

Bowie and Don finally arrived at the bottom of the staircase, both breathing heavily. Mason squatted down and took a quick look. The prosthetic leg was completely missing, but Don was uninjured.

"Can you get up these stairs?" he asked.

"Hell, yes!" Don rolled onto his belly and started high-crawling up the stairs.

Mason looked over at Bowie.

"Get up there," he directed. The dog took off up the stairs, flying past Don to search for Vince and Father Paul.

Men began climbing through all three windows, and another loud crash sounded from the back of the church. The enemy was coming.

Backing up the stairs, Mason laid down suppressing fire, and convicts dove for cover. He was the last to arrive at the top of the stairs. The other three men were already clustered at the end of a long hallway. Vince was wrapping a pillowcase around his injured hand.

"Where?" Mason asked, looking to Father Paul.

"I . . . I don't know. The dormitories won't hold."

Mason spied an open doorway to a small cast iron spiral staircase leading up to the steeple.

"There!" he said, pointing. "We'll fight from high ground."

Bowie took off up the stairs, barking as he went, and the men followed. Despite having to crawl, Don was nearly as fast as any of them as they made their way up into the steeple.

A loud *whoosh* followed by a *boom* sounded from outside in the street. It was followed by two more. The steady pounding of gunfire stopped, giving Mason and his team time to navigate the stairs and secure a heavy trapdoor behind them.

The steeple was an open-aired bell tower that measured about fifteen feet across. A large church bell was hanging at the center with a donut-shaped walkway surrounding it. The railing was only about four feet high, and the men could see out into the cold night. Several cars were now on fire in front of the church, the yellow flames licking up into the darkness like the tongue of a rising Balrog. Chief Blue had given them their diversion.

Father Paul began to say a prayer. "Dear Lord, rescue us from—"

Mason placed a hand on the priest's shoulder.

"Father, while we appreciate your plea to the heavens, the time for prayer has passed. Now is the time for men to act."

He nodded. "What can I do?"

Mason looked around. The floor of the steeple was only about ten feet above the roof, making it possible for him to lower and drop. Bowie wouldn't make it, and neither would Vince nor Don with their injuries. Father Paul was a maybe, but there was no point in sending him down into the fray.

"I need you to ring the bell just as you did the other day. Let the town know we need their help. Vince, you and Don stay here and protect him."

Father Paul smiled and tears formed in his eyes.

"Of course. We will send out God's call, and they will come."

Mason wasn't so sure, but he didn't put his doubts into words.

"You're going over?" asked Vince.

"I've got to get Rommel."

Detecting that his master was about to do something without him, Bowie inched closer. Mason squatted down next to him and cupped his hands on either side of the dog's head.

"You can't come this time. I need you to watch over these brave men."

Bowie whined and pressed hard against his chest. Mason kissed Bowie on the nose before pushing him away. Then, without another word, he climbed over the railing and dropped to the roof below.

storm was brewing. Thick clouds rolled in from the west, and the wind tossed trash around the interstate like it was the empty fairgrounds of a departed carnival. Tanner and Samantha had made their way to a community called Perimeter Center in the northeast corner of Atlanta. It had been a long, hard day, and both were physically exhausted. A loud boom of thunder sounded, and they instinctively reached for one another.

"We need to get indoors," she said, looking up at the dark sky.

He pointed ahead to a large shopping mall that was a good quarter mile away.

"Let's see if we can make it there."

"Okay," she said over the wind. "But we'd better hurry."

Within minutes, the bottom dropped out. Rain blew over them in huge sheets, forcing Samantha to hold on to one of Tanner's belt loops to keep from losing him in the deluge. After nearly half an hour of walking through the soaking rain, they arrived at the mall. The doors to a JC Penney were already broken in, and the two stumbled in wetter than survivors of a shipwreck.

"You okay?" he asked, water spraying from his lips.

She coughed. "I think so."

He sat down on a small bench and poured water out of his boots. Looking over at her, he couldn't help but smile.

"You look like a drowned cat."

She flopped down next to him.

"Well, you look like the monster from the black galloon."

"Black galloon?"

"Yeah, it's from a scary movie."

He smiled. "Now I remember."

"This place looks creepy," she said, looking around at what was left of the clothing store. Daylight extended into the small entryway, but, beyond that, it was dark and cold. Body parts from mannequins were scattered on the floor, like the whole place had been staged for a slasher film involving teenagers and chainsaws. Piles of clothes, many with tags still attached, were sitting on counters and draped over racks, the wishful thinking of an optimistic retailer. The air smelled of decomposing bodies, but thankfully the store was large enough to diffuse much of the stench.

"It's better than being out there," Tanner said, gesturing outside. Rain continued to pour, and cracks of lightning lit the sky like flashes from the cameras of overzealous tourists.

"I don't know. I've got a bad feeling about this place."

"Come on," he said, standing up. "Let's see if we can find something dry to wear."

A few minutes later, they stood in the dark trying on clothes. They each had a small penlight they had found in a store outside the prison, but neither of the lights worked very well.

"What do you think?" Samantha asked, clicking on her penlight. She was wearing orange bellbottom pants and a white shirt with beaded buttons and puffy sleeves.

"Not bad for a hippie."

"What's that?"

"A hippie is someone from my generation. They sort of lived for the moment."

"So, is that good or bad?"

"Given that it's the end of the world, I'd say it's perfect."

She looked down at her clothes one more time and then smiled, apparently satisfied with her selection.

A loud noise sounded as something fell from within the store.

Samantha's eyes grew wide, but she didn't say a word.

Tanner brought up the shotgun.

"Kill the light and move close to me."

They stood in the dark for more than two minutes just listening. Nothing moved.

"I don't hear anything," she whispered. "Maybe something just fell—"

They both stiffened as they heard the unmistakable sound of feet trudging across the carpeted floor. Samantha grabbed Tanner's arm. He could see the light from the store's entrance about forty yards away, but further into the store, there were only indistinguishable shadows.

He leaned down to Samantha and whispered, "Make yourself as small as possible."

She sank down, curled into a ball, and leaned back into a rack of clothing.

Tanner took three large steps away from her and clicked on his penlight. Something lunged at him. Perhaps it had been a man at one time, but not anymore. It was hunched over, arms dangling in front, its hands twisted like a gargoyle's claws. The face was disfigured with pus-filled blisters, and its eyes leaked black slime.

Tanner froze for a moment as if caught in the gaze of a basilisk. The creature latched onto him, its claws digging into the flesh of his neck, its mouth closing in toward his face. He instinctively struck forward with both hands, the shotgun and flashlight falling from his grip. The creature stumbled back, howling with uncontrolled fury.

The shotgun had fallen at Tanner's feet, but he dared not try to pick it up. Instead, he stepped forward and stood over it. The monster jumped at him again, spitting and screaming as it lurched forward. This time Tanner was better prepared. He sidestepped and hit the creature with a hammer strike to the back of its neck. It stumbled to the ground, but before it could fall, Tanner grabbed it by the ear and lifted it back up. Latching onto its windpipe with his other hand, he ripped its throat out.

He dropped the corpse and quickly retrieved his shotgun and flashlight. Holding the two together at waist level, he spun in a circle. Several other creatures were approaching, each as hideous as the first. He fired at the closest, and it folded backward like a cardboard cutout. Others rushed toward him, screaming and hissing as they came.

Tanner shucked the spent shell and racked and fired another. The pellets tore a softball-sized hole through the hip of the closest creature. Tanner racked another shell, but before he could get it off, they were on him.

Disfigured hands beat and clawed, bruising and tearing his flesh over and over again. He wrestled the shotgun free and fired, sending another one of them stumbling back. Unable to work the shotgun's action, he whipped it up, striking a fourth one under the jaw. The stock split its face open as bone splintered through flesh.

Hands pulled at him from behind. Tanner planted his feet and spun around hard with the shotgun. It caught another creature on the side of its head, knocking it to the ground. It struggled to get back up, but he racked a shell and put an end to it. It was only then that he realized he was no longer being attacked. His adrenalin was pumping so hard that he couldn't tell whether he had killed all of the creatures or if some had retreated back into the darkness.

His ears were ringing from the thunderous shotgun blasts, and his body stung from a dozen different wounds. He racked a fourth shell and

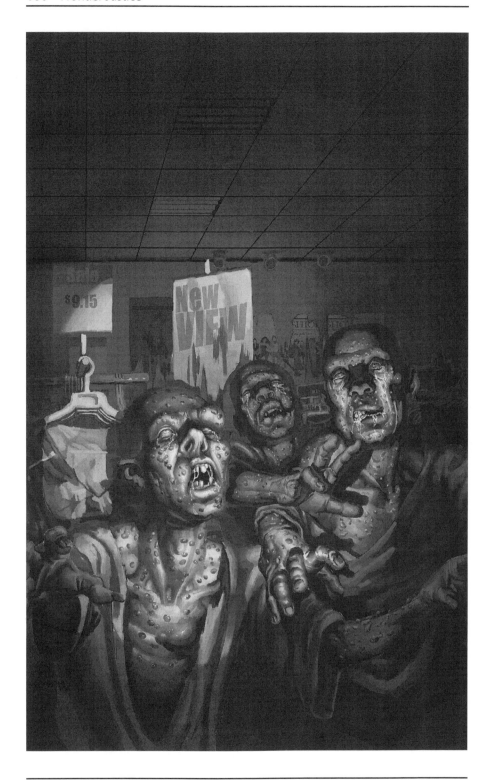

searched the darkness around him. His penlight lit only a few feet in front of him, but there was nothing still alive in the beam.

Tanner stumbled back to the rack in which Samantha had hidden. Before he could say anything, she peeked out from between the clothes.

"Can we go now?"

❧ ❦

Tanner sat on the tailgate of a large four-wheel drive pickup parked in front of a liquor store. Samantha used a rag soaked in vodka to clean the bites and scratches covering his arms and neck.

"Do they hurt?" she asked, dabbing one of the wounds.

"Not really."

"They sure look like they hurt."

He took a swig of lukewarm beer.

"I suppose you're waiting for me to say you were right."

"About?"

"About not going into the store."

"Well, I was right."

"Yes, I suppose you were."

"Were they zombies?"

He sighed. "Of course not. They were just people."

"They didn't look like people. They looked like zombies."

"If they were zombies, then we have a big problem."

"What?" she asked, setting the rag aside and looking at her nursing handiwork.

"They bit me. You know what that means."

Her eyes grew wide.

"Do you feel . . . hungry?"

He rubbed his stomach.

"Now that you mention it, I'm starving. I have a strange craving for red meat. The rarer the better."

She furrowed her eyebrows.

"Seriously? Don't mess with me."

"I'm seriously hungry. Aren't you?"

"Well, yeah."

"There's a supermarket just up the street. I bet we can find something to eat there."

"You're going into another store?"

"What have I got to lose? I've already joined the walking dead."

"Good point."

"How about we get food and then find a safe place to sleep?"

"Okay, but if you start to change . . ."

He took another swig of beer.

"Don't worry. My ex-wife would tell you I'm incapable of change."

℞ ℟

Tanner and Samantha knelt behind an overturned ambulance. The gurney had fallen out the back door, but thankfully, it was empty. They stared at a Safeway supermarket directly across the street. In front of the store was a lone child riding on a tricycle, whizzing up and down the sidewalk as if warming up for a jump with Evil Knievel. He couldn't have been older than four, and yet, an adult was nowhere in sight.

"That's strange, right?" she said.

"I'd say."

"You think his parents are inside?"

"I hope so."

"He couldn't have survived all alone." She paused. "Could he?"

Tanner shrugged. "Let's go check it out. But keep your eyes open."

"I'm going to walk behind you just in case someone shoots at us."

"Great. Thanks for thinking of me."

As soon as they stood up and stepped clear of the ambulance, the little boy spotted them. He whipped his tricycle around and raced into the entrance to the grocery store. They approached slowly, studying the windows and doors to see if anyone might be watching. Tanner carried his shotgun in one hand by his side so as not to appear any more threatening than he already did. When they were a few steps from the store's entrance, a teenage boy stepped out. He had a deer rifle pointed at them.

"Stop right there," he said, holding up the rifle.

They stopped.

"What do you want?" he demanded.

"We're just looking for some food."

The young man looked over his shoulder and said something to someone inside the store. After a moment, he turned back to face them.

"My mom wants to know where you're coming from."

"We drove over from Alabama." Tanner walked slowly toward him as he spoke. "We're traveling all the way to Virginia. What about you folks?"

The teenager started to back up but quickly found himself with his back pressed against the wall of the store. He seemed uncertain about what to do next.

"We're from here." He looked over his shoulder again, and by the time he looked back, Tanner was standing close enough to brush his teeth.

Tanner glanced into the store and saw an attractive woman holding the toddler who had been riding out front. He nodded to her, and she returned a nervous smile. He turned back to the young man and extended his hand.

"I'm Tanner." He motioned behind him. "And this is Samantha."

The boy lowered his rifle and reluctantly shook Tanner's hand.

"I'm Lucas. Mom?" He looked back at her again for her approval.

She came out of the store, carrying the young boy.

"I'm sorry," she said. "We're afraid. That's all."

"He won't hurt you," said Samantha. "Tanner only kills bad guys and zombies."

The woman looked confused. Tanner indicated that Samantha had a screw loose by rotating his finger beside his head. The woman smiled and nodded.

"What are you folks doing here?" he asked.

"Like you, we came to get food," she said. "That was nearly a week ago. We just ended up staying here. There's plenty of food and drink, and we really didn't have anywhere else to go. I'm Janice, by the way." She reached out and lightly shook his hand. When she pulled her hand away, he felt the gentle swipe of her fingers across his palm.

"We're waiting for my dad to come back," added Lucas.

"I suppose a grocery store is as good a place as any to hole up. How long has your dad been gone?"

"Three days," he said. "So he'll be back anytime now."

"My husband went out to gather supplies," she added. "He was going to the mall and a gas station."

"The mall," Samantha whispered, tapping Tanner on the side of his leg.

"I see," he said, ignoring her. "And have you seen other survivors?"

"A few cars here and there. No one has bothered to stop."

"You're lucky," said Samantha. "We've seen all kinds of bad things."

"She's right. You have been lucky. I wouldn't advise letting your boy ride out in plain sight like that."

"That was an accident," she said. "We're normally more careful. Come on, let's get inside."

As they stepped into the store, Tanner and Samantha were immediately struck by the smell of rotting food. She covered her nose and started to gag.

"Wow, that's bad."

"You get used to it," said Lucas.

Janice and Lucas led them around the Safeway as if giving a tour of their family's new vacation home. To Tanner's surprise, the store was still fairly well stocked. Long shelves were stacked with canned and boxed foods, as well as soda and bottled water. The right side of the store was filled with piles of rotting fruits and vegetables, with huge clouds of sour flies swarming around the produce.

"Now I know what stinks," said Samantha.

"That's only half of it," said Lucas. "The refrigerated foods at the back of the store are worse. We try to stay clear of that area because of the flies and maggots."

Janice cut her eyes at her son.

"Sorry about the smell," she said, touching Tanner's arm. "But there's still plenty of good food left."

"And you're sure you wouldn't mind us having a little?"

"Of course not," she said, smiling. "Lucas, go find something for Tanner and his daughter to eat."

Samantha started to say something, but Tanner reached out and put his arm around her.

"Thanks, we'd love a good meal. We've been eating junk food for two days. My baby girl needs her protein if she's going to grow up big and strong."

Samantha pinched his palm, hard.

Janice set her little boy down. "Tommy, stay closer this time."

He nodded and raced toward his tricycle. Within seconds, he was pedaling off down one of the aisles.

"Boys," she said.

Tanner smiled. "He's young enough that he'll adapt to this mess. Probably better than the rest of us."

She reached out and took his arm in hers.

"Come on, let's sit and have a little grown-up talk. Your daughter can go with Lucas if she wants."

Tanner looked over at Samantha.

She squinted at him.

"Yeah, Dad, that's fine." She turned and followed Lucas deeper into the store.

Janice took Tanner to a small area on the far wall where she had set up makeshift sleeping quarters for her family. Blankets were piled on the floor, paper plates were lying everywhere, and several plastic lawn chairs were set out in a small circle. She led him to one of the chairs, and then slid another up next to his.

"So, you're headed to Virginia?" she asked, pulling her hair back and tying it in a small bun.

"That's right," he answered, not quite able to take his eyes off of an open button on her shirt.

"Family there?"

"The little girl's mother."

"Your wife?"

"No, we're not together."

"I understand," she said. "Relationships come and go, but our children are forever."

"I am having a hard time getting rid of her," he said with a chuckle.

"Poor thing. You're hurt." She leaned over and touched one of the cuts on his face.

"Believe me. They got the worst of it."

"I bet they did. You look like a man who can take care of himself. But even a big, strong man needs a woman's touch from time to time. Am I right?"

Having spent more than four years in prison, Tanner was certainly not immune to Janice's charm.

"Where I came from, women were in short supply."

"And you missed them?"

"Oh yes."

She stood up and moved over to sit on his lap. For a moment, he thought that the flimsy chair might collapse, leaving him with a sore backside and her a red face. Fortunately, it held. And, while Janice's clothes and face were dirty, her body was warm and inviting. He felt a powerful desire that had been bottled up longer than the fizz in Vernor's ginger ale.

"I'm a practical woman, Tanner," she said in a soft voice. "I know that if my sons and I are to have any chance of surviving, we're going to need a man around here. A big, strong man."

"What about your husband?" he asked, his eyes directly in line with her breasts.

"If he was still alive, he'd already be back." She leaned in and kissed one of the cuts on his forehead.

Not only did Tanner know that she was probably right about her husband, he also didn't feel the need to argue the point when she was riding sidesaddle on him. The best he could muster was to restate the obvious.

"We're going to Virginia."

She lowered her kisses to his cheekbones.

"I know you are. But there's nothing saying you have to go right away."

He closed his eyes and enjoyed the soft touch of her lips on his skin.

"I gave my word."

She put her lips to his ear.

"We all have to break promises sometimes," she whispered. "Lean back and let me see if I can't change your mind."

ॐ ॐ

Lucas pushed a shopping cart up one of the aisles while Samantha followed a few paces behind him.

"So what grade are you in?" he asked.

"Sixth."

"That's cool. I was in eleventh. I guess I won't graduate now. No college either."

She shrugged. "It's just school."

"Yeah, but I really wanted to go to college. It's the only way to be someone important. Now, I'm stuck living in a grocery store. That's not fair, you know?" He pulled down some cans of potted meat from one of the shelves and dropped them in the buggy.

"If you don't mind, get some of that tuna for me," she said. "I like tuna." He grabbed several cans and stuffed them into her backpack.

"I had plans, dreams. I was going to get my degree, drink beer, meet a girl. The whole college experience. You're young, so you don't really get it. But believe me, this whole thing blows."

"Tanner says you have to accept things the way they are. Deal with hardships without getting caught up in the unfairness of it all."

"No offense, but that's just stupid grownup talk. Parents don't want to admit how bad things really are because they figure we'll freak out or something." He knocked a box of crackers into the cart. "Why do you call your dad by his first name, anyway?"

"Oh, that. Well, we didn't live together for a while. I had another dad, you know?"

"Ah, I get it. The whole stepdad thing."

"Right," she said, nodding.

"Well, when my dad gets back, we're going to get out of here. That's for sure."

"Where are you going?"

"To live on the beach in Florida. I figure we can move into one of those big mansions on the water. Everyone's dead, right? No one would care anymore. Besides, teenagers like warm weather where they can skateboard and stuff. Any young people who are still alive will probably go there."

"That sounds nice. But what if your dad doesn't come back? Three days is a long time to be gone."

He whipped around and stared at her like she'd just kicked him in the shin wearing a pair of steel-toe boots.

"I told you," he said. "My dad's getting supplies. What the hell do you know anyway?"

There was a dark hatred in his eyes that scared Samantha. She looked around, but they were completely alone. She wasn't even sure that Tanner would hear her if she screamed.

"Sorry," she said. "I'm just a dumb kid."

He stared at her, clearly deciding her fate. Then, as if he had taken a swig of Dr. Jekyll's potion, the darkness vanished as quickly as it had appeared.

"That's okay," he said, turning back to his shopping. "Anyway, you'll like my dad. He's real smart and takes good care of us. My mom and I both love him to death."

❧ ❧

Tanner was zipping up his blue jeans when he heard Samantha and Lucas approaching. Janice was a few feet away, scrambling to get her blouse buttoned.

"That was amazing," she said, winking.

"No complaints here either."

Lucas rolled up, pushing a shopping cart full of food.

"I brought a little of everything. Meats, potato chips, peanut butter . . . take whatever you want."

Tanner picked up a box of granola cereal, tore open the top, and started munching on a handful.

"Thank you. We appreciate the generosity." He looked over at Janice. "We really do."

"You know what they say about southern hospitality," she said, grinning.

He opened his pack and loaded up several cans of food.

Looking over at Samantha, he said, "Did you get what you wanted?"

She patted her backpack. "I'm good, but it'll be dark soon. We should really be going."

"I suppose you're right," he said, looking out the window.

"What? I thought you were going to stay with us. The food . . . the hospitality." Janice seemed beside herself.

"While we appreciate your kindness, we can't stay. We have to get to Virginia."

"But you said . . ."

"No, darlin', I didn't."

Her face turned red with anger.

"This isn't right."

He slung his pack over his shoulder.

"I agree. That's one reason we're moving on. Give your husband a few more days. If he doesn't show, I suggest you try to team up with other survivors. You'll fare better that way."

"Why does everyone keep saying that?" Lucas said through clenched teeth. "My dad is coming back."

"I hope you're right." Tanner motioned for Samantha to head out of the store. She seemed eager to lead the way.

As he turned to follow her, Janice blurted, "Take us with you."

Lucas spun around. "Mom, we can't leave. Dad won't know where to find us."

"Take us with you," she pleaded. "I'll take good care of you. And Lucas will be a great big brother to your daughter."

Lucas crossed his arms and pressed his lips together, refusing to say another word.

It took Tanner longer than it should have to decide.

"I'm sorry, but I can't do that."

"Why? We won't be any trouble."

"I know you won't," he said, not entirely convinced of his words.

"Then why?"

"The truth is there are people out looking for us who wouldn't hesitate to kill you and your sons. Believe me. You're safer here."

"But . . ." She searched for the right words that would change his mind. Not finding them, she sighed and said, "Okay, I get it." She stepped forward and gave him a small hug. "No regrets," she whispered in his ear.

He smiled and kissed her cheek.

"You take care of your boys."

She stepped back and put her arm around Lucas. As if on cue, Tommy reappeared on his tricycle from around one of the aisles.

"I'll do whatever it takes to keep my family safe," she said.

Tanner turned and followed Samantha out of the store. Of all the things Janice had said to him, her last few words were surely the most telling.

🙢 🙠

The Super Star motel was nothing special. The beds were lumpy and the carpets stained. Following a meal consisting of canned fruit, tuna fish, and peanut butter, Tanner and Samantha had retreated to the abandoned motel in hopes of getting a decent night's rest.

Most of the rooms were free of bodies, which Tanner attributed to people avoiding bedbugs, even when the end of the world was at hand. Samantha had already fallen asleep on one of the beds. The room was dark but safe.

He stepped out onto the porch and sat in a folding lawn chair. Cigarette butts were scattered on the ground like pages of a lost diary. He opened the last remaining beer and took a drink. It had been a hell of a day. As he sat listening to the quiet of the night, the deep rumble of diesel engines sounded in the distance. A few minutes later, a long caravan of lights traveled along the bypass around Atlanta.

Were they the ground forces that Agent Sparks had mentioned? Were they looking for Samantha? He had no way to know for sure.

He leaned around and looked in through the doorway at the sleeping girl. She hadn't moved. He rubbed his eyes, weighing his actions of the past two days. What was he doing? Taking Samantha halfway across the country was about like trying to get Dorothy back to Kansas. He couldn't begin to answer why he had agreed to do it. She wasn't family. Not only that, she brought with her some very serious baggage, the type that might land him back in prison.

He turned around and leaned back in the chair, watching the convoy of military vehicles slowly pass in the distance. It would have been easy to draw the soldiers' attention. Perhaps firing a shot into the air or flashing a car's headlights. But he did neither. Instead, he sat quietly in the dark until the convoy passed, the string of tail lights shining through the night like landing beacons on a runway. He took another long swig of warm beer. It tasted awful, but hell, it was still beer.

The flames from burning cars cast shadows that danced on the blacktop like stoners at a psychedelic rave. Mason had managed to remain undetected as he climbed down from the roof and took cover behind a nearby car. The sound of the church bell ringing reverberated across the town, its chimes pleading for any who heard it to take action.

From his vantage point, he could see that the lower floor of the church had been overrun. The gang of convicts now came and went freely through the front door, which had been propped open with the body of one of the men who had died in the street. Standing just inside the entrance, Rommel personified the general whose name he had stolen, barking orders to his men, his head held high with an air of victory. Convicts moved all around him, so getting any sort of a clean shot at their leader was all but impossible. Even if Mason could have pulled one off, in doing so, he would have given up his position, and, therefore, his life.

He keyed the radio and whispered, "Chief Blue, are you there?"

No answer.

"Chief?"

The only response was two quick pops of the chief's radio. That likely meant that either the enemy was close or that the chief was injured. Either way, he was out of the fight for now.

The radio sounded again, and Coon's voice crackled.

"Marshal, are you boys still kicking in there?"

Mason was relieved that Coon had not been caught or killed.

"We're still alive," he said. "I made it off the roof and am going to engage at street level. Can you help?"

"You betcha. I'm on the roof of the diner to the northwest."

Mason looked toward the diner to see if he could spot Coon, but the firelight made it impossible to see anything above street level.

"I'm going to try to draw Rommel out. I'm counting on you to put a bullet in his eye."

"Will do, Marshal. Once that happens, it's gonna to get pretty hairy down there. You'd best be ready for a fight."

"Understood. Stand by."

There was a sudden burst of gunfire from the bell tower. Ten or more rounds were fired in quick succession followed by two unmistakable booms of a shotgun. Vince and Don were trying to hold the roof.

Mason knew that they couldn't hold out for long in the steeple. If the bell stopped ringing, it would mean he had failed them. His attention was so firmly set on the events happening at the church that he didn't notice a figure stealthily approaching from behind. By the time he heard the footsteps, it was too late. Powerful hands grabbed him by the shoulders and threw him onto his back. Mason's rifle was knocked from his grip, and a dark figure fell upon him, pounding with heavy fists.

He struggled to free his pistol, but his attacker was not only relentless, he was also skilled. Then, as quickly as it had started, the beating stopped. The man pulled back, his blanket-covered face barely perceptible in the darkness.

Mason reached for his Supergrade but stopped when he recognized his attacker.

"You!"

"I'm sorry," Erik mumbled, pulling the blanket up so that it shadowed his disfigured face. "I didn't know it was you, Marshal." As before, his words were muffled and difficult to understand. "We came to help."

Mason leaned over and spat out a mouthful of blood.

"Who came?"

"Six of us. Survivors."

"You came to fight against the convicts? But why? I thought the townspeople had cast you out."

"They did, but if the town falls to the lawless ones, we'll be killed for sport. Just like you, we fight for our survival."

Mason rubbed his jaw, which was already starting to swell.

"You pack a solid punch."

"I was a bouncer back in the day. I know how to hurt people." There was an unmistakable sadness in his voice.

"Do your people have guns?"

"Yes."

Mason thought for a moment. He had no idea of how much help they could offer, but six more guns firing at the enemy couldn't hurt.

"Okay, let's do this."

"What can we do to help?"

"Get your people in positions where they can do the most damage, and wait for my signal."

"And then?"

"Let all hell break loose."

⇛ ⇝

Time was Mason's worst enemy. He would have preferred a more tactical approach, perhaps picking off the convicts one at a time and then disappearing back into the darkness like a covert assassin. As it was, he had minutes at best before they overran the bell tower, killing the priest, the deputies, and his dog.

He had to draw their attention away from the church, and, more important, Rommel out into the open so that Coon could get a clean shot. The only way to do that was to convince them there were more important things to worry about than the folks holed up at the top of the bell tower.

Before he could adopt a course of action, three sets of headlights approached from the east, stopping a block away from the church. A dozen convicts scrambled to take up positions behind cars facing the new arrivals.

Steve Price and his two grown sons clambered out of the first vehicle and sought cover, hunting rifles in hand. Two more men, unknown to Mason, exited the second car. The third vehicle roared past the other two and drove directly up to the barricade that the convicts had set up with their own cars.

Ava stepped from the car with her hands raised high into the air. Mason felt his gut twist into a knot. What in the hell was she doing?

"Don't shoot!" she yelled. "I have an offer for Rommel!"

One of the convicts motioned for her to come forward while another ran to the church to inform him of what was happening outside. Within seconds, Ava was surrounded and pushed toward the church. To Mason's dismay, rather than luring Rommel out, the men ushered her inside.

With most of the convicts' attention now on Steve Price and his men, it was easy for Mason to shuffle from car to car to get closer to the church. He got near enough to see through one of the large windows that Father Paul had smashed out.

Ava was speaking to Rommel with her back toward Mason. He couldn't hear what was being said, but her hands were out as she made an impassioned plea. After a brief conversation, Rommel turned to say something to Slim and then swung back and backhanded Ava hard across the face. She went down and didn't get back up.

Mason had no idea what she had offered, but, whatever it was, Rommel wasn't buying. What he would do to her next wasn't clear, but Mason couldn't stand by and watch it happen. He had to buy everyone some time. Mason did the only thing he could. He started shooting.

His first shot hit a convict standing guard directly in front of the entrance. The man fell back against the church's massive door, leaving a trail of blood like mucus from a giant banana slug. Mason shifted his aim to several others standing near the church. Four more shots and three more hits, only the last bullet going wide as that man dove for cover. Mason continued to fire until his rifle was out of ammunition, sending convicts scrambling for cover and randomly returning fire in every direction.

The sound of rapid gunfire caused the men facing off with Steve Price to open fire as well. Each side cut loose, sending hundreds of rounds in opposite directions but hitting very little. A group of six convicts surrounded Mason's position, pinning him down with a sustained barrage of heavy fire. Glass and shrapnel exploded around him, as if they had blasted a cannon loaded with grapeshot.

Maintaining cover behind the car, he held his rifle high in the air with both hands.

"I surrender!"

Everyone stopped firing long enough to see what was going to happen next. Even Rommel and Slim moved to look out the window of the church.

The convicts slowly approached Mason, weapons at the ready. As they got close to him, he stood up and tossed his rifle so that it skittered noisily across the blacktop in front of them. Everyone's attention briefly shifted to the weapon, and Mason drew his Supergrade and started firing again.

His shots were so rapid that they sounded like *pops* from an unbroken string of firecrackers. A few of the convicts returned fire, but none were trained well enough to keep a steady hand in the face of death. By the time the Supergrade's slide locked to the rear, all six convicts who had approached lay bleeding in the street. Mason had taken only a grazing bullet wound to his left shoulder.

He looked over to Rommel whose face betrayed both concern and uncontrolled rage. Suddenly, Rommel's left eye exploded in a pink puff of blood. He fell backward, out of sight. Coon had taken his shot.

A cacophony of screams erupted. The men inside the church were screaming for help. Steve Price and his men were screaming to advance. The convicts all around the street were screaming as they started taking fire, seemingly from every direction. Most of the bullets missed their targets, but they had the desired effect of turning the street into a true battle zone.

Convicts cowered behind cars or ran off into the night. Perhaps ten remained in the street fight, and Mason knew they wouldn't last long. He slapped a fresh magazine into the Supergrade and ran for the church. Several bullets whizzed by close enough for him to feel the unmistakable vibration of their passing, but none broke skin. He wasn't sure if it was enemy or friendly fire, but it didn't really matter. A bullet was a bullet.

He made it to the door of the church, and, without breaking stride, burst into the room. The scene inside was as chaotic as that on the street. Slim knelt beside Rommel, trying desperately to stop the bleeding from the back of his head. Three other convicts were lined up at the windows firing out into the street, exactly as Mason and his deputies had done. Ava lay unconscious in the center of the room where she had fallen.

Mason fired three quick shots as he dove behind one of the pews. The first took the ear off one of the men at the windows. The second and third shots punched holes in the same man's chest. As Mason hit the floor, the wooden pew splintered, as the two remaining convicts returned fire. To avoid the worst of it, he squatted down and shuffled along the back of the pew. A bullet grazed the top of his head, leaving behind a burning pain and a steady trickle of blood flowing down the side of his face.

When he had progressed about ten feet, Mason rose up just enough to sight over the pew. He took two more quick shots. Both hit the closest man, who was busy reloading his rifle. The last shooter scrambled along the open floor, desperately seeking cover. Mason steadied his aim and shot the convict in the side of his head.

The room fell silent.

Mason stood up and faced Slim. He was holding Rommel's large revolver out before him like a religious offering. It was aimed at Mason, but he seemed uncertain about what to do next. Without hesitation, Mason shot him in the face.

A barrage of gunfire sounded from upstairs. A fight for the steeple was underway. He dropped out the partially spent magazine and slapped in his last remaining one. Weapon held firmly in front of him, Mason turned and raced up the stairs.

A convict stood at the top of the stairway, but his attention was on the door to the steeple. Without slowing, Mason fired twice, both bullets striking the man in the chest. He fell dead without ever knowing who had shot him.

Mason stopped at the top of the stairs, unaware of a convict standing at the small doorway to the steeple staircase. Seeing his partner drop, the man turned and let loose with a blast from a sawed-off shotgun.

Mason barely had time to drop to the ground before the buckshot tore apart the wall and bannister. Lying on his side, he fired three shots up at the man. The first splintered his femur, and the other two caught him in the gut as he fell. He lay on the ground, moaning and crying from the pain. Mason took one final shot, and the man fell silent.

He scrambled to his feet and rushed down the corridor toward the steeple's doorway. Sounds of heavy gunfire came from within. He holstered his Supergrade and scooped up the shotgun from the fallen convict. He ejected the empty shell and chambered another. There was no easy way to tell how many rounds were left in the shotgun. He could only hope it would be enough.

Standing to one side, he peeked around the doorway. The spiral staircase was crowded with men queued up like paratroopers preparing to breach an enemy bunker. The man at the top was firing blindly through what little remained of the trapdoor.

Mason fired the shotgun up into the stairwell. A thunderous volley of buckshot pellets spewed out. He pumped round after round, firing as quickly as he could bring the heavy weapon back on target. When the shotgun finally locked open, he took it in his hands like a baseball bat and charged up the stairs, swinging it down upon any who still moved.

When Mason was finally finished, he stumbled to the bottom of the staircase and flopped down with his back against the wall, his feet splayed out into the hallway. The smell of gunpowder and blood mingled like a graveyard aphrodisiac.

He checked his Supergrade. Three rounds remained in the magazine, plus one in the chamber. He set it on his lap and waited. He had inflicted a lot of damage to be sure. Whether it was enough or not, only time would tell. Four rounds left. If any more than that were needed, the fight would be lost.

He closed his eyes, intending only to rest them for an instant.

When Mason finally opened his eyes, a large tongue was lapping the blood from his cheek. He raised his arms and hugged Bowie's massive head, the dog's unmistakable breath washing over him. Father Paul was standing behind Bowie, looking down at Mason with a concerned face.

"Thank God you're alive."

"Is it over?"

"Yes."

"Did we win?"

Father Paul looked around at the pools of blood and spatter of gore lining the walls.

"No one won, but we fared better than these unfortunate souls."

Mason reached out and held tightly to the dog.

"Help me to my feet, boy."

Bowie stood firm, and Mason used him as a makeshift crutch to get to his feet.

"How are Vince and Don?" he asked, fearing the worst.

"Both alive. You just missed them."

"And you? Are you hurt?"

Father Paul looked himself over.

"It appears that God has seen fit to spare me yet again."

Mason suddenly remembered Ava lying unconscious on the floor.

"Ava's downstairs. She needs attention."

"Easy there," Father Paul said, catching Mason as he swayed. "Vince and Don have already taken her to the hospital. I expect that she'll have a good shiner for a couple of weeks, but otherwise she should be fine. Looking at that gash on your head, the hospital should be your first stop as well."

Mason took a few steps to test how surefooted he was. The floor didn't come rushing up to greet him, so he figured he would make it. He left Father Paul to lament over the loss of life while he went to sort things out downstairs. The bodies of Rommel, Slim, and the other convicts lay where they had fallen. Steve Price and his two sons were coming in through the front door. One of the young men had a blood-soaked bandana tied around his calf.

Mason nodded to them.

"I appreciate what you men did."

All three looked shaken but were holding themselves together for one another if nothing else.

"It became a bloodbath in the end," said Steve. "I'd be surprised if a single convict is still alive."

"Probably better that way." Mason walked past them, patting the youngest of Steve's sons on the shoulder as he passed.

King Street looked as if it had been the target of a suicide bomber. Dozens of bodies were draped over cars or lying in the street as lifeless contortions. A large group of townspeople was busy with the cleanup, although Erik and the other virus survivors were conspicuously absent. Now that the shooting was over, there were more than enough hands for what had to be done. Fires would be put out. Bodies would be removed. Blood would be hosed from the church walls.

Coon leaned against a nearby car, his hunting rifle propped up beside him. He nodded at Mason.

"That was a good shot."

"Not really."

"Why do you say that?"

"I was shooting for the other eye." He extended a hand, and Mason shook it. "It's been an honor, Marshal."

"For me as well."

Coon took the badge off his shirt and held it out to Mason.

"I think you can find someone more fitting to pin this on."

Mason reached out and closed Coon's hand around the badge.

"I doubt that."

"All right then," he said, shrugging. Without another word, he picked up his rifle and walked slowly away into the night.

Mason looked around for Chief Blue but couldn't find him anywhere. He asked several people, but the answer was always the same. No one had seen him since the shootout started.

He keyed his radio.

"Chief Blue, sound off."

At first there was no reply, and then came several quick pops on the radio.

"We're coming, Chief. Hold on." Mason called over a young man who was helping with the cleanup. "You hold this microphone button down and keep talking into the radio."

"Okay, sir, but what should I say?"

"Sing us a song."

"A song?"

"Son, we just won a battle. A little music is in order."

"Yes, sir."

The young man paused for a moment and then began to sing.

Oh, say can you see . . .

Mason smiled. The national anthem seemed fitting enough.

He quickly gathered a few volunteers to help scout the immediate area. Using the singing to guide them to Chief Blue's radio, they eventually found him lying behind the counter in an ice cream shop. There was blood everywhere. Two convicts lay dead on the floor, and another was draped over the counter as if helping himself to another scoop.

Mason knelt down to inspect the chief's wounds. He was conscious and in intense pain.

"You did good."

The chief blinked in response.

Mason found three bullet wounds, one in his chest, one in his right thigh, and one through the side of his neck. Of the three, the one through the leg looked the most serious. The bullet had nicked the femoral artery, and he was bleeding out.

Mason slid off the chief's belt and cinched it around his thigh to stem the flow of blood. The bleeding slowed but didn't completely stop. Chief Blue was having trouble breathing, sucking in air with a gurgling sound, like he was trying to breathe through a wet pillowcase. Mason rolled him onto his side, and the chief's breathing immediately improved. He held Chief Blue's hand and leaned in close.

"Chief, I need you to listen to me. You took a bullet to the chest that has most likely pierced a lung. A second bullet passed through your neck, which probably hurts like hell, but doesn't look serious. Finally, a third bullet opened your right femoral artery. I've stopped the bleeding from your leg, but you've already lost a lot of blood. Now, I need for you to make a decision, a really tough one."

Chief Blue stared up at him, tears forming in his eyes.

"I need you to decide whether you want to live or die. If you want to live, you're going to have to fight for it. If you're willing to die the hero you are right here on this floor, I'll stay with you until you pass. You just let me know if you've got anything left in you."

Chief Blue squeezed Mason's hand.

"Okay, then. Let's do it."

He turned to the men who had helped him find the chief.

"One of you help me carry him. The other run ahead and get a vehicle ready for us. We're headed to the hospital. Now move!"

Mason slouched in an oversized leather chair that pulled out into a one-person sleep sofa. Bowie rested in a huge furry pile at his feet, snoring softly. A few feet away, Chief Blue was lying on a hospital bed, an intravenous tube dangling from his arm to a bag of clear liquid. He was looking intently at Ava, who stood next to the bed studying his medical chart.

"Am I going to make it, Doc?" he choked out in a gravelly voice.

She shrugged. "Hard to say."

Chief Blue smiled. "Doc, your bedside manner needs some work."

"With enough rest, you'll be fine," she said, squeezing his shoulder. "We recovered the bullets and largely repaired the damage. But you're going to need a couple of weeks of bed rest and even more months of taking it easy. Give your body a chance to heal properly, okay, Chief?"

"Believe me. My wife will insist on it."

Ava looked over to Mason.

"How's my other patient?"

He touched the scab that had formed on his scalp.

"Tender."

"That's not a word anyone would ever use to describe you." Her face was serious. "What you did was . . ." She closed her eyes and, for a moment, he thought she might cry.

"I'm fine, Ava. You know that better than anyone. A graze here." He touched his scalp again. "Another one here." He gently rubbed his shoulder. "They're nothing."

She nodded, tears welling in her eyes.

"Yes, but an inch here or there, and we'd have lost you."

He stood and put his uninjured arm around her.

"I'm fine," he repeated. "How's your eye?"

She touched the edge of the large bruise surrounding her left eye.

"A reminder to stop being stupid."

He kissed her eye very gently. In turn, she kissed him on the lips. Then she pulled back and straightened her doctor's coat.

"Okay, then. I have more patients to check on." As she swung the curtain aside to leave, Don and Vince stood waiting like kids outside the principal's office. "Well, go on," she said, "but keep it short. The chief needs his rest."

Don had repaired his prosthetic leg and was back on two feet again. Both men had an assortment of small cuts peppering their faces.

"You two look like you gave mouth-to-mouth to a bobcat," said Mason.

"What are you talking about?" said Vince. "We look great."

They all laughed.

"When they blew the rooftop door, we both took a face full of splinters," explained Don. "Missed the eyes, thankfully."

"That was good work holding the tower." Mason looked from one man to the next. "It took a lot of grit." Embarrassed, they both looked to their feet.

"I can only speak for myself," said Vince, "but I was as afraid as a six-year-old schoolgirl facing a pack of wild dingoes with nothing more than a squirt gun."

Don snorted and rolled his eyes.

"You should have heard him bellyache over a little hole in his hand, and there I was with an entire leg missing!"

They laughed again. Chief Blue closed his eyes in pain.

"Please . . . please," he begged.

Don reached out and patted Vince on the back. "Jokes aside, my man and I, we held it together."

"I'm proud to have fought beside you men," said Mason.

"Same for us, Marshal. I've never met anyone with more raw fight in his spirit. That was some hard stuff you did."

Vince and Chief Blue both nodded their agreement.

Mason thought of the dead he had left behind. Despite the terrible brutality he had inflicted on his enemy, he felt only a sense of relief at seeing his friends alive. War had always been that way.

"Thankfully, that's behind us now."

"The battle may be over, but we still have to put this town back together. Any chance we might convince you to stick around?"

Mason stood and shook each man's hand.

"It's been an honor, but I have another road to follow."

&❧ ❦

The scene at the Church of the Fallen Saints was one of repair and cleanup. More than a dozen people were busy spackling the walls, others were patching the door, and still others were clearing away debris from where the back wall had collapsed.

Mason and Bowie stood out front. The street had been cleared of the dead, but blood was spattered everywhere like the stains of a huge paintball fight. Father Paul came out to greet them.

"I wondered when you'd be coming by," he said with a warm smile.

"The whole town seems to have come out to put your church back together."

He looked over his shoulder.

"Indeed. It's more of a landmark now than ever before. A place where few stood against many. Daniel Boone would have been proud."

"What about the back wall? That's going to be tough to fix."

"Steve Price has already started gathering supplies. He assures me that it's a few days' work, no more."

"Anything we can do to help?" Mason asked, patting Bowie on the side.

"I think you've both done more than your fair share." Father Paul knelt down and gave the dog a big hug. "You take care of this man, and he'll take care of you." Bowie licked the priest's face and wouldn't stop until he stood back up.

Wiping his face with a small handkerchief, Father Paul said, "Next time you come this way, please stop in to check on us."

"I will."

The two men shook hands and then hugged. Father Paul gave Mason a long look.

"I have a feeling that your work is only beginning. May God go with you on what I'm sure will be a most difficult journey."

℘ ℘

Ava leaned close to Mason, her hand resting on his leg as he steered the truck slowly through the wreckage of Highway 321. Bowie was asleep in the bed of the truck.

"This was a great idea, getting away."

"We could both use a few days of rest," he said. "Besides, you'll enjoy the cabin. It has some amenities you probably haven't had for a few weeks."

"Like electricity?"

"Exactly."

"And hot water?"

"That, too."

"I love it already."

"I'm curious about something. What did you say to Rommel in the church?"

She touched her swollen black eye.

"Ah, that."

"Yeah, that."

She paused for a moment.

"I was just trying to get them to spare everyone."

"I know. So?"

"So, in exchange, I offered to take them to the hospital and hand over our medicines."

"You were willing to trade the town's medicines for our lives?"

"Not really."

"But you said—"

"It was a bluff, that's all. We hid the bulk of the hospital's medicines more than two weeks ago in case there was a break-in. I was going to lead them to the hospital to give you time to escape, regroup, or whatever it was you needed to do. Things were looking pretty bleak."

"They'd have killed you for that."

"No," she said. "They'd have done worse."

"Please don't feel the need to do anything so womanishly stupid in the future."

She lifted her head in defiance.

"*Womanishly* stupid? Is that even a real word?"

"If it's not, it should be," he said, laughing.

Before she could come up with a suitable retort, he motioned for her to look ahead. A caravan of large vehicles was approaching from the opposite side of the highway. At first, he wondered if it might be Carl Tipton and his group of RVs.

Ava sat up straight, pulling her hands to her lap. Mason unlatched the rack that held his rifle in place.

As the vehicles got closer, they saw that it was a military convoy: four HMMWVs and a large, plated van. The lead HMMWV sped ahead of the others and swerved sharply into Mason's lane. Four soldiers jumped out, wearing battledress uniforms and gas masks, and carrying assault rifles. They quickly set up a defensive position behind their vehicle.

Mason eased his truck to a stop about thirty feet from them and rolled down the windows. He re-latched his rifle rack, and removed his Supergrade from his hip and placed it on the floorboard out of sight. Then, he opened the window to the truck bed and told Bowie to lie down and be quiet.

Two soldiers carefully approached his truck, one going to each side, rifles at the ready. The remaining soldiers maintained their position behind the HMMWV. The rest of the convoy came to a stop about a hundred feet behind the lead vehicle.

A soldier stepped up to the truck window, his rifle pointed directly at Mason's head.

"Identification," the man demanded, his voice muffled by the thick rubber mask. He extended a hand covered in a black latex glove. Mason handed over his Marshal's badge and identification. The soldier glanced at the badge, unimpressed.

"Her too," he directed.

Ava passed her hospital badge to him. The soldier put their identifications into his front pocket.

"Step from the vehicle."

"Is this really necessary?" asked Ava. Mason looked at her and shook his head.

Seeing the look in his eyes, she nodded and opened her door. The soldiers pressed them against the hood of the truck and then searched them carefully. When they were satisfied they had no weapons, they motioned for the rest of the convoy to approach.

A second group of soldiers advanced, carrying portable electronic equipment. All the men were wearing gas masks. A man with a gold oak leaf on his hat led the way.

"I'm Major Gacy of the Viral Defense Corps," he said after inspecting and returning their identifications. "As authorized by Executive Order 16661, you will be tested for the Superpox-99 virus. This will be administered by a certified viral determination specialist. Do you have any questions about the test that is about to be conducted?"

"You've developed a portable test to determine if a person has the virus?" asked Ava.

"Yes. It requires only a quick sampling of your blood. A simple finger prick."

"And if we refuse to be tested?" asked Mason.

"We will exercise our authority to forcibly test you."

"I suspected as much."

"Will you consent to be voluntarily tested, or are other measures necessary?"

"Given our choices," Ava said, not hiding the disdain in her voice, "of course we'll consent."

Major Gacy motioned for one of the medical specialists to approach. He carefully took Mason's hand and inserted his right index finger into a small disposable box. Once his finger was inside, the soldier clicked a small switch at one end, and a spring-activated needle lanced Mason's fingertip. The specialist handed the blood box to another man beside him who inserted it into the chamber of an electronic gadget about the size of a Polaroid camera. After about ten seconds, a green light showed on the unit's display.

"Clear," he said, removing the sample from the unit.

He then moved over to Ava and repeated the process. When the needle pricked her finger, she winced slightly but said nothing. The soldier passed the blood box back to his partner who once again inserted it in the pathogen-testing device. After a slight delay, the light on the unit again turned green.

"Clear." Major Gacy motioned for everyone to lower their weapons and remove their masks.

"It should have been obvious that we don't have the virus. We don't have any of the symptoms." Ava pulled up her sleeves. "No blisters on the skin; no hemorrhaging of the eyes; no fever."

"Yes, ma'am," said the major, "but we're also ensuring that you aren't simply a survivor of the virus."

"Have you seen the survivors? You'd have to be blind not to be able to tell a survivor from someone who hasn't been exposed or is simply immune."

"It's my job to be sure, ma'am." The major turned to leave.

"Why would it have mattered anyway?"

He stopped and turned back.

"Excuse me?"

"Why would it have mattered if we were survivors? They aren't contagious anymore."

"That's correct."

"So, why even test them?"

"Since you specifically asked," said Major Gacy, "I'm required to inform you that some of the survivors of Superpox-99 have been shown to experience violent paranoia. We are, therefore, advising people who have not been infected to stay clear of them."

Ava tried to recall her encounters with those who had been infected.

"I guess I could believe they act a bit paranoid, but they didn't seem more violent than anyone else."

"Not yet perhaps, but my superiors report that many of those infected will eventually become quite dangerous."

"Major, what exactly is your mission?" asked Mason.

Major Gacy stood up straight.

"As part of the VDC, my mission is to help ensure the recovery of our nation from the worst pandemic in history."

"And how exactly are you doing that?"

"Under Executive Order 16661, I have been instructed to euthanize any and all who have been infected with the virus."

Ava and Mason stood dumbfounded.

"My God, you're killing the survivors?"

"We have strict rules—"

"You're murdering innocent people," she said, suddenly short of breath. "Our government is killing its own citizens."

"We're following orders," he said, flatly.

"Men have hidden behind those words before," said Mason. "It doesn't usually end well for them."

Major Gacy's lips tightened, but he said nothing. Instead, he turned and motioned for the soldiers to return to their vehicles. Within seconds, they were loaded and moving down the highway toward the town of Boone.

Mason and Ava watched as the armored convoy maneuvered through the wreckage of cars until it eventually disappeared from view. Tears filled her eyes as she reached out and held onto his arm.

"I don't belong in this world."

He smiled and shook his head.

"You're wrong, Ava. This new world isn't for men like Major Gacy or me. We are but a means to an end. Eventually, a time will come when people like you and Father Paul will help to right this nation."

"And until then?"

He pulled her close and stroked her beautiful black hair.

"Until then, we must fight and we must love with every bit of passion left in our souls."

"I don't know if I can do that."

"You've already proven that you can."

"Tell me that things will get better."

"They will."

"But they'll never go back to normal, will they?"

"Not in our lifetimes, no."

"I'm afraid."

He kissed her on the forehead.

"Then lean against me and know that I'll keep you safe."

She laid her head against his chest, comforted by the slow steady beat of his heart. Perhaps the old world had ended, but a new one was just beginning.

ONLINE INFO

For information on my books and practical disaster preparedness, see:

http://disasterpreparer.com

CONTACT ME

If you enjoyed this book and are looking forward to the sequel, send me a short note (*arthur@disasterpreparer.com*). Like most authors, I enjoy hearing from my readers. Also, if you have time, perhaps you would be kind enough to post a positive review on Amazon.com.

I frequently travel the world giving disaster preparedness seminars. If you are a member of a church, business, or civic organization and would like to sponsor a disaster preparedness event, please keep me in mind.

Best wishes to you and your family!

FREE NEWSLETTER

To sign up for the *Practical Prepper Newsletter*, send an email to:

newsletter@disasterpreparer.com

Do you have a Plan?

Ninety-nine percent of the time the world spins like a top, the skies are clear, and your refrigerator is full of milk and cheese. But know with certainty that the world is a dangerous place. Storms rage, fires burn, and diseases spread. No one is ever completely safe. We all live as part of a very complex ecosystem that is unpredictable and willing to kill us without remorse or pause.

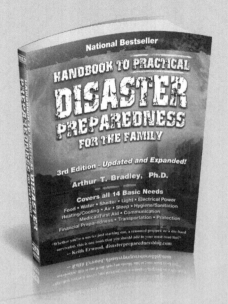

This handbook will help you to establish a practical disaster preparedness plan for your entire family. The 3rd Edition has been expanded to cover every important topic, including food storage, water purification, electricity generation, backup heating, firearms, communication systems, disaster preparedness networks, evacuations, life-saving first aid, and much more. Working through the steps identified in this book will prepare your family for nearly any disaster, whether it be natural disasters making the news daily (e.g., earthquakes, tornadoes, hurricanes, floods, and tsunamis), or high-impact global events, such as electromagnetic pulse attacks, radiological emergencies, solar storms, or our country's impending financial collapse. The new larger 8" x 10" format includes easy-to-copy worksheets to help organize your family's preparedness plans.

Available at Disasterpreparer.com and online retailers

Learn to Become a PREPPER

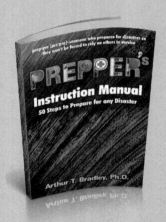

If your community were hit with a major disaster, such as an earthquake, flood, hurricane, or radiological release, how would you handle it? Would you be forced to fall into line with hundreds of thousands of others who are so woefully unprepared? Or do you possess the knowledge and supplies to adapt and survive? Do you have a carefully stocked pantry, a method to retrieve and purify water, a source for generating electricity, and the means to protect your family from desperate criminals? In short, are you a *prepper*?

This book comprises fifty of the most important steps that any individual or family can take to prepare for a wide range of disasters. Every step is complete, clearly described, and actionable. They cover every aspect of disaster preparedness, including assessing the threats, making a plan, storing food, shoring up your home, administering first aid, creating a safe room, gathering important papers, learning to shoot, generating electricity, burying the dead, tying knots, keeping warm, and much more.

Recent events have reminded us that our world is a dangerous place, whether it is a deadly tsunami, a nuclear meltdown, or a stock market collapse. Our lifestyle, and even our very existence, is forever uncertain. Join the quickly growing community of individuals and families determined to stand ready.

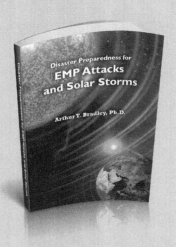

Made in the USA
San Bernardino, CA
13 August 2014